TRUST THE LIAR

TRUST THE LIAR

Susan Zannos

Walker and Company
New York

First published in the United States of America in 1988 by the Walker Publishing Company, Inc.

Published simultaneously in Canada by Thomas Allen & Son Canada, Limited, Markham, Ontario.

Library of Congress Cataloging-in-Publication Data

Zannos, Susan.
    Trust the liar.

    I. Title.
PS3576.A55T7   1988   813'.54   87-31802
ISBN 0-8027-5697-2

Printed in the United States of America

10 9 8 7 6 5 4 3 2 1

For my favorite writer:
A. L. Tate, my father.

TRUST THE LIAR

1

I HAD SENT a call slip for Brandon to come to my office to discuss the matter of his detention time. Also the matter of his cutting classes. Which was why he had detention time.

"I have to go to work after school," he said. "I have a wife and five children to support."

"Brandon, that is ridiculous. You do not have a wife and five children."

He looked very serious. "No, really, I do."

"Brandon, you are fourteen years old. The human gestation period is nine months. Even allowing for unusual sexual precocity . . . "

"Three of them are adopted."

"Brandon, I do not want to play. I do not want to understand you. I do not care if you are emotionally deprived, culturally deprived, educationally deprived, or plain rotten. I just want you to follow the rules. You have cut classes. You have detention time. I will expect you at three-oh-five in room one-oh-eight."

"This is probably the last chance I'll have to see my brother. He's dying of leukemia."

"Brandon, you do not have a brother. According to your records, you are an only child. I wish you did have a brother. I wish that he were an only child."

"My father was trapped in the mine when the shaft collapsed and . . . "

"Brandon!"

"Right. One-oh-eight in room three-oh-five."

1

He grinned at me and ducked out the door. I kept the scowl on my face until he was gone, and then bent over the next batch of call slips. Brandon Henshaw was one of the few bright spots in my job, which was attendance monitor at Fair Oaks High School. The job itself was an experiment being conducted by the local school board in response to a number of pressures. For one thing, the parents felt the school was not taking enough responsibility in keeping tabs on the students. For another, the teachers had won, as a bargaining item in the last contract negotiations, release from extra duties such as detention room supervision. For a third, the state was refusing to pay for specially funded programs if the students were not actually in attendance during a given class period.

I guess the experiment was a success. More or less. The school administration thought so, and the teachers seemed to agree, and most of the parents appreciated knowing immediately if their kids missed a class. The trouble was that after six months of the school year all the solvable problems had pretty much been solved. The theory that having to face immediate consequences would convince kids not to cut school was a sound one. By mid-November it had generally sunk into even the thickest sixteen-year-old skull that ducking out of American history to play Donkey Kong at the 7-11 wasn't really worth three hours of detention time after school, and that if the detention time wasn't completed the next step was suspension from classes and the devil to pay at home.

Now we were down to the unsolvable problems. The kids I was currently working with were mostly young people trapped in family games that were removing all their options: you can't win; you can't break even; you can't get out of the game. Human misery ran so deep through the substratum of Fair Oaks society that to speak seriously of detention time as a punishment was idiocy. I had given my letter of resignation to the principal's secretary that morning.

It was the last class period of the day, so after getting Tim Jordan's call slip back—as usual he had cut afternoon classes—I headed for the detention room. Brandon came in just as the final bell rang. He stood in front of my desk and waited for me to look up from my attendance forms and acknowledge his presence.

"Where are your books, Brandon? You know you have to have something to study or read."

"You're not going to believe this—"

"Right."

"—but I think my best friend has been kidnapped."

"That is highly unlikely since no one . . . well, never mind. Just get your books and sit down."

I hadn't finished my sentence because I realized that what I was about to say was merely true. No one would pay a nickel for either Brandon or his best friend or both of them together. His friend Felipe was one of the Mexican kids from the labor camp, although not one that I had ever lured into the high school. Which was one reason why Brandon's visits to these halls were at best sporadic.

"I have to get my books from my locker."

"Hurry up."

He didn't come back. I was surprised, since on the days Brandon did come to school he went the extra mile. That is to say he went through the whole day of school and then stayed for detention. He knew, and I knew, that his detention time, if completed, would last until he was 112 years old. But Brandon understood about matters of form.

Why I considered Brandon Henshaw one of the bright spots in the job was not clear to me. Certainly he was not among my successes. Certainly he caused me a lot of uncomfortable moments as various members of the teaching and administrative staffs scheduled conferences to speak solemnly about "the Brandon Henshaw problem." As they saw it, there were ramifications beyond the immediate hassle of trying to keep Brandon in school: as long as the other students were aware of Brandon's relative freedom of movement, they would be tempted to imitate him. Brandon was in fact due for immediate suspension, after which it would be decided whether he would be transferred to the Open School program, a loosely organized boondoggle for kids who weren't quite bad enough for reform school, weren't quite stupid enough for remedial or custodial institutions, but who wouldn't conform to the rules of the regular high schools.

The clock crept toward four o'clock. At each minute the long hand moved a half minute back, as though getting a run for the big leap, and then clacked a minute forward. Every six minutes the shorter hand slid half a minute forward. There was a flurry of discussion among the group at three-fifty about whether they deserved the infrequently awarded ten minutes off for good behavior. I ruled that they had met only half of the requirements for this dispensation: they had been quiet—but they hadn't been studying. There was a one-minute grumble, nine minutes of glazed boredom, and then the bell rang and freed us all.

Don Marquez, the principal, was waiting for me when I put the attendance records in my office. He had my letter in his hand.

"Carrie, please think about this," he said. "You're doing a fine job. Your system works. The kids respond to it without resentment because it's consistent and fair. And the parents are very impressed. You're certainly making my job easier, and the amount the school district is saving on state and federal funding more than pays your salary. At least think about it for a couple of weeks."

I just shook my head. They didn't need me to keep the system working, and Don knew it. His usual technique for getting what he wanted consisted of fulsome praise followed by emotional blackmail. He was well started on the first, so I was curious about the form the second would take.

"Look, Carrie, I know it's hard. But look at it this way—you're finding out about situations that no one realized existed. County medical services were able to help the Borchers, and no one would even have known the mother was ill if you hadn't gone out there to see why Terry Sue was missing classes."

I shook my head again. "I don't want to find out, Don. I just don't want to know. I'm sorry. I never should have stayed in Fair Oaks after Rick was killed."

I walked out of the building into a gusty March wind blowing across the school lawn. Dark clouds were scudding across a lowering sky. My car, another bright spot in my life, was one of the last ones in the staff parking lot. Volumes have been written about the symbolic value of automobiles in America, and I could have added at least a chapter to any of them about the complex pleasures my Mercedes afforded me. The big one was remembering Rick—not remembering that he was dead, but remembering that he loved me enough to accept that car from his father because I wanted it. I could still hear him:

"Carrie, a car like that is an outrage! Nobody needs a couple tons of conspicuous consumption to get from one place to another—especially when the people you're driving by probably don't even have enough to eat."

I don't think he really understood why I wanted it, but he understood that I did want it, and that it had something to do with living in Fair Oaks, with the long hours he put in at the clinic, even with the fact that he didn't want it. It *was* an outrage. I smiled as I slid behind the wheel. That was the whole point in a way. The world you look at through the subtly tinted windshield of a new Mercedes is a different world than you see through the cracked windshield of an old VW. And the way people treat you when you get out of that Mercedes and leave it at the curb is different than the way they treat you when you get out of the VW. I didn't make that true, and I wasn't going to pretend that it wasn't true. Rick was only embarrassed by the car for a little over six months.

I was going to drive out to the McGraw place and talk to Tim Jordan's dad. I'd talked to Mr. Jordan on the phone twice, and both times he'd said he'd have a talk with Tim and Casey, but nothing had changed. Casey wasn't a serious problem, although he could be if he was influenced by his brother's habits. The younger of the two brothers, Casey was a tall, good-looking blond basketball player, a Tom Sawyer type—although without the civilizing influence of an Aunt Polly. Still, his popularity with the other kids and with his teachers made his days at school pleasant enough that he made it through most of them. Evidently he hadn't that day. His name showed up on the last-period absentee list.

It was Tim I couldn't connect with. Tim was hard-core Huck Finn and didn't have any use for school. A year older than Casey, he was in the same class—both of them sophomores—because a broken leg had made him miss most of the ninth grade. He didn't seem to have any close friends; he just hung around on the edges of the jock crowd that Casey ran with. At the present accounting, he wasn't receiving a passing mark in any of his afternoon classes. I'd talked to him several times and was pretty sure it wasn't because he couldn't have gotten good grades if he'd wanted to. I wanted to see if there were any clues I could pick up from talking to his father.

6

It was unlikely that Sam Jordan would be in before five or five-thirty, so I decided to drive by Brandon's house, even though I didn't particularly expect that he'd be there. The Henshaw place was a battered frame house sitting at the back of a weed-overgrown lot. Rusting machinery and discarded furniture parts poked through the weeds. A buckling and broken cement walk bisected the lot and led to the decaying porch leaning out from the first floor of the oddly tall and narrow structure. The house looked like it had been designed to squeeze between houses on either side, except there were no houses on either side. The Henshaws' neighbors lived in relatively new ranch-style homes set close to the street, and called or wrote to various town and county officials at intervals in an attempt to force Virgil Henshaw to clean up his property.

The yard was a showplace compared to the inside of the house. I didn't want to go to the door, but I did want to find Brandon, so I got out of the car and made my way along the walk to the front porch. I had been inside the house once. I'd come about noon one day and Brandon had opened the door. I'd talked my way in, and despite my claims that I'd already seen everything, I was shocked. My nose was shocked, at least. I didn't want to go in again. On that first visit Brandon's father had been in a drunken stupor on the sofa. I thought he was at least half awake, but by feigning unconsciousness he avoided talking to me. Brandon was mute with misery at having me enter his private hell. Why is it that we can endure almost anything except having someone else know about it?

This time the door opened before I stepped onto the porch, and Virgil Henshaw came out. Brandon's father looked twenty years older than he probably was. The effects of advanced alcoholism and attendant malnutrition had destroyed his health to the extent that it was impossible to imagine what he might have looked like when he was young and well.

The bleary eyes slid away without meeting mine. "You're from the school, ain't ya? You been havin' trouble with that boy again? I talked to that boy an' told him he was gonna get the whippin' of his life if he missed classes. He been missin' classes again?"

"Is Brandon here, Mr. Henshaw? I'd like to speak with him if he is."

"Naw, he ain't here. I thought he was in school. Ain't he in school today? I'm gonna give him the whippin' of his life if he ain't in—"

"School is over for the day, Mr. Henshaw. I just wanted to speak to Brandon for a minute."

"Naw, he ain't here. I gotta get to work now. You have any trouble with that boy, you just let me know. I can handle him all right."

When I got back into the car my hands were trembling on the steering wheel. Even the tinted glass couldn't do much for Brandon Henshaw's place, his life. I decided to stop by the 7-11 to see if Brandon and Felipe were playing the video games. They weren't, and no one who was had seen them, so I got a Styrofoam cup of coffee and took a short drive out into the country. I liked to drive out along the dirt lanes bordering the orchards, stop the car, and think about what my life was going to be like after June thirtieth. That was the magic day when I would lock the door of my apartment for the last time, hand the keys over to someone else, put my suitcase and a couple of boxes of books and records into the trunk, and head for San Francisco. This whole ridiculous aberration, this accidental detour into small-town America with all its grotesque charms—like Virgil Henshaw, like the labor camp, like being truant cop for Fair Oaks High, like walking into the clinic that August night and seeing that the reason for it all had been knifed and was bleeding his life out onto the white tile floor—was just a rather prolonged anomaly in my existence.

My reality had nothing to do with this place. My reality was in San Francisco, where it had always been waiting for me. My reality was efficient and clean, private and rather exclusive. Sure there were sensitive fourteen-year-old kids in the world who had to live under conditions that it was illegal to impose on animals—I was sure I could get the SPCA to take Virgil Henshaw's dogs away from him for maltreatment, which would at least improve Brandon's living situation to the degree that it would eliminate the dog shit and rotting dog food from the kitchen, where the poor animals were penned. My hands were shaking again. I was supposed to be thinking about San Francisco, not the Henshaw kitchen. Sure there was a lot of misery in the world, but I didn't have to look at it, and I didn't intend to.

That was a difference Rick and I had never resolved. Maybe we would have, someday, if we'd had time. Maybe it would have torn the marriage apart eventually. I'd never know that. Sometimes we argued about it, sometimes we joked about it—I said it was because he'd grown up in the activist save-the-world era of the sixties and he said it was because I'd grown up in the passive me-first era of the seventies—but it had always been there between us. It wasn't theoretical. I wanted Rick to leave the clinic where he took care of migrant workers and join his father's successful practice in San Francisco. He wouldn't.

Most of the time it wasn't a very large problem. We liked the same things, and each other. We liked the same music, the same people—usually people who were a little tipped, who were passionately involved with some activity or cause or idea—peanut butter and banana sandwiches, buttermilk, Robert Altman films, sitting up reading until nearly dawn. And even if we hadn't liked the same things, the physical attraction had been so intense and immediate and overwhelming when we met seven years ago in Berkeley that we probably would have married even if we hadn't spoken the same language.

Although we had blow-ups —I'd want to drive into San Francisco to go to the opera or to a play, and at the last minute he wouldn't be able to go because another baby was being born to a family that already had ten children and no income—we never stayed mad long. But we did get mad sometimes, and when we did we were aware enough of each other's vulnerable places that we knew how to get at them. I'd tell him that it wasn't altruism that kept him in Fair Oaks, but knowing that he'd never be the doctor his father was. He'd tell me that my only interest was in his family's money.

I didn't like to remember those arguments. I particularly didn't like to remember that the last time I'd seen Rick alive had been one of those times. We'd been on the way out the door to go to Harriet McGraw's lawn party when the telephone rang. We'd had a tussle at the door.

"What telephone?" I'd said. "I don't hear any telephone. You've been working too hard, you're hearing buzzing sounds in your ears," and tried to keep him from going back.

But he did, dragging me with him in the crook of one arm while he answered the phone. "I'll meet you at the clinic," he said into the phone, letting me go.

"Oh, not again," I said. "What if it had been three minutes later? We'd be on the way to the party and they'd have survived somehow."

"Carrie," he said, and his voice had that righteous smarminess that enraged me, "the boy's in pain. It won't take long, and then we'll go to Harriet's. We'll be fashionably late. You know she won't mind."

"No," I said, "I'll drop you at the clinic and go alone.

10

I'm not into playing the doctor's noble little wife tonight. I want to be with people who are good enough at what they do that they don't have to give it away."

I knew that Rick was a good doctor. But I also knew that he never thought he was good enough. I drove him to the clinic, where the Velasquez family were already waiting in their old Plymouth truck, saw Rick's bearlike profile in the rectangle of light from the door when he switched on the light and stood waiting for the others to go in first, and didn't return the wave he gave me as I drove off.

I didn't go to Harriet's. I drove past, saw the lanterns strung around the rose garden and the moving shapes that were guests on the back lawn, and went back to the apartment to wait until I thought Rick would be done and we could go together. I'd started reading, and waited too long. . . .

I finished my coffee, and looked down the row of peach trees. They'd leaf out soon, and then they'd be blossoming, great soft pink billows that would gradually sift to the ground like warm snow. Then the fruit would form, hard little green pods that would swell and ripen through the hot summer into fat blushing peaches, smooth and furred and delicious. And then they'd fall from the trees and rot. The crop wasn't even worth picking. The canneries were closing one by one. Peaches didn't freeze well, and nobody bought canned fruit anymore. Not in this country and not from this country.

Well, where was Brandon, anyway? Not at home, not at the 7-11. Maybe he was out at Felipe's house in the labor camp. I had plenty of time, so I drove over there. I was used to the pressure of the dark eyes watching when an Anglo drove into the camp. The houses were double bungalows of cement brick covered with flaking green paint. In the windows hung bright tablecloths, sheets, sometimes even a plastic curtain to keep out the sun and the curious eyes of the neighbors. The Ramos's front window was distinguished by a worn orange chenille bedspread stretched across it, fringe looping down from the rod it was pinned to. A young woman opened the door a crack when I knocked. She had a baby in her arms and a toddler hanging onto her skirts.

My Spanish wasn't very good, but good enough to ask Felipe's whereabouts. She said he wasn't there. I asked her if she'd seen Brandon Henshaw, and she shook her head. At the same time, behind her, I saw Brandon walk into the room, where four other children were watching cartoons on television.

"Well, actually, she probably didn't see me. She's Felipe's aunt—Mrs. Ramos. I've been in the back room with Felipe's brother," he said. "We're getting ready for our parachute mission into—"

"Brandon, I want to talk to you."

Mrs. Ramos stepped back, her eyes wide and apprehensive. Brandon spoke to her in his soft Spanish, rapidly and gently. I didn't catch it all, but he apologized for frightening her, and said that I was a friend and she shouldn't be afraid of me. Then they were talking about Felipe and I could see that Mrs. Ramos was starting to cry. She turned away from the door and lowered her voice. Brandon spoke with her in a low voice, and then came out and closed the door behind him. We both got into my car. He ran his fingers over the dashboard.

"Nice car."

"Yes. Yes, it is. And I'm going to get a nice life to match it. I'm going to get a job to match it, and an apartment overlooking the bay to match it, maybe in Sausalito, and—"

"Good idea. You've been by my house, haven't you? I don't know why you do that, it just upsets you."

"Doesn't it upset you?"

12

"It's just a cover for our counterespionage operation. A few more weeks and we'll have captured Abu Hudanit, the key Palestinian terrorist organizer, and I'll be moving on."

"Brandon . . ."

"OK if I play a tape?"

"Sure. They're in a box under your seat."

He studied the rows of cassettes silently for a few moments. "These are all classical music, aren't they? I don't know what any of them are. You pick one."

I reached over and tapped Glenn Gould playing Bach toccatas and Brandon slipped it into the tape deck. He looked out the window at the orchards sliding past as the amazing notes changed all the world to beauty. After the first side, Brandon ejected the tape and looked at it.

"Do you like it?" I asked without taking my eyes from the road. Then I looked at him, at the wonder in his eyes. "Sorry," I said. "Dumb question."

"Where are we going?" he asked. "I've got to go out to the McGraw place. We're headed in that direction."

"That's where I'm going. I have to talk to Sam Jordan. I thought maybe you could ride along and we could talk afterward. What are you going out there for?"

"I'm not even sure, but Felipe hasn't been home since yesterday morning, and the last time his brother saw him he was starting to cut across the McGraw place, walking by the river down through the hay fields. They were going over to see if it's time for the rice planting in the flats."

"Why didn't Alfredo go with him?"

"You know Felipe. He said they could get to the highway quicker by going along the river, and Alfredo said it was quicker along the road, so Felipe bet him a dollar's worth of quarters for the video games and crossed the fence right about here. Could you stop and let me out, please?"

"It's nearly dark. What are you going to do thrashing around out there in the dark? Why don't you wait until tomorrow?" I had stopped the car just on the other side of the bridge, but I didn't want Brandon to disappear again.

"Mrs. Pritchard, you know I can't miss school tomorrow."

"Brandon, sometimes you go too far, you really do."

"You don't believe me, do you?"

"Look, I believe that something's going on, and that Felipe's missing and his aunt is worried about him. I certainly don't think he's been kidnapped. And I certainly don't think you're going to find anything down by the river when it's getting dark. What kind of harebrained notion is that?"

"Well, Felipe doesn't have any place to go but home, and there's no reason he wouldn't want to. I mean there isn't any trouble in his family. So either something happened to him, or somebody is keeping him somewhere, right? I want to go down along the creek because there are all those old shacks down there from when the migrants used to have to live on the owner's property before they built the camp."

"So you think if anybody's down there, they'd have a light?"

"Or a fire or something."

"I can't believe this, Brandon. I can't believe I'm sitting here getting drawn into one of your fish stories. Why don't you just come along while I talk to the Jordans and then we'll talk about it afterward."

He shook his head. "Look, I'll meet you right here at the bridge in half an hour. But I've got to go down there. Really." He got out of the car, jumped across the ditch, and crawled through the double strand of loose barbed wire that kept the peach trees from getting out and wandering down the road.

14

2

THE JORDANS LIVED in a big frame house that had formerly been the McGraw home. It was set about three miles from the highway on a gravel lane that formed a part of the road system of the McGraw Orchards. Jensen McGraw and his wife lived in Fair Oaks now, and in their San Francisco townhouse, their Cancun condominium, and such other residences as the bush league wealthy might have at their disposal. "Bush league" because I guess there are a lot of millionaires around nowadays. It's not the big deal it used to be. Anyway, they no longer lived in the old McGraw family home set back in the orchards. Sam Jordan was the resident factotum. He had literally hundreds of acres of orchards, hay fields, and outbuildings to oversee, not to mention all of the machinery to keep in repair, so Jordan was nearly impossible to reach by telephone.

As I pulled up to the place, I saw a half dozen men standing around the raised hood of an ancient pickup truck in the open area in front of the house. It was nearly dark, and the truck was illumined by the circle of light from a single powerful bulb that dangled from a pole leaning out from the fence. I wondered what the Jordans did with a house that large, and decided, from the boarded-up windows on the second floor, that they probably lived in the kitchen and a couple of rooms on the main floor, shutting the rest off. According to local gossip, Sam Jordan's wife had run off when the boys were still toddlers, leaving him with the abiding dislike of women that he had evidently communicated to Tim, although not, perhaps, to Casey. At any rate Casey was frequently seen in the halls at school with one or another admiring young beauty dangling from his arm.

The Mercedes captured the attention that had formerly been invested in the truck's innards, and the men stared as I got out of the car. A large man left the group and moved toward me, not bothering to smile. Tim Jordan followed him.

"Mr. Jordan?" He nodded. "I'm Carrie Pritchard, attendance monitor at the high school. I wonder if I could talk to you for a few minutes?"

He nodded again, and I waited for him to indicate some place where we could speak privately. Instead, he turned and nodded toward Tim. "I figure we're going to be talking about Tim," he said, "so we won't be saying anything that docsn't concern him."

Father and son were a formidable bastion against my intrusion into their world. Sam Jordan wore gray striped mechanics' overalls, well marked with grease, that stretched over an imposing bulge of belly. The McGraw logo, the surname on two leaves and a round fruit, was on the pocket. Jordan's receding hairline no longer reached to the white line where the leathery skin of his face had met the hat he must have worn in the sun. Tim stood beside him, a slight boy who would never reach his father's height or girth, but who equaled his massive resistance to forces attempting to alter his chosen course.

"OK," I said, "Tim has been cutting his afternoon classes. Since the beginning of this month he's been leaving school at lunch and not coming back. He has a lot of detention time building up because none of these absences have been excused."

"He's been working for me in the afternoons," Sam

16

Jordan said. "I need him here. We've got a lot of machinery to take care of."

"I've got a job to do, too. My job is to see that young people in this school district are conforming to the state laws governing education. Tim isn't."

Sam Jordan gave a slight shrug, indicating that the laws governing education in the State of California were not high on his list of priorities. I saw the slight twitch of smile pull at the corner of Tim's mouth, and understood his lack of response to my exhortations. The Jordans' world seemed tight and solid. And I liked it. As far as I could see, Sam Jordan had done a good job raising his boys. Casey was doing well in his chosen activities, and now that I saw Tim out here in his world of engines and pickup trucks and farm machinery, it seemed that he was fine, too.

"I don't see any problem with the situation," I went on. "Tim's probably learning more working with you than he would be in auto shop classes." The auto shop teacher was also the football and basketball coach, and his interests were firmly focused on competitive sports.

Jordan looked bored and I felt silly. He was not going to soften up for a little flattery. "I'd like to make out an application for a work-study program for Tim," I said. "Basically all it would mean is that he'd be doing what he is doing now but getting credit for it toward his high school diploma. Jensen McGraw would need to sign it as employer, and Tim would have to attend morning classes, but he's been doing that fairly regularly."

"What about the detention time?" Tim asked.

"As long as we're working out a program with your father's approval, there won't be any question of detention time."

"Even the time I already got?"

"That's up to your father. If he wants to put it in writing that you missed school because you were work-

17

ing here, then that's all I need for the files. Otherwise, the absences are still against your record."

"What about it, Tim?" Sam Jordan asked his son. "You want to fool with this work-study business?"

Tim looked around the open area, his glance taking in the vehicles and machinery waiting to be worked on. He had his hands in the back pockets of his Levis. I realized that it was entirely his choice to come to school at all, that as far as his father was concerned he could be working here mornings too if he wanted to. "I don't know, Dad. I guess so. I guess I'd like to graduate if I can."

Sam Jordan nodded again, a man who had brought up his boys to think for themselves, and who wasn't going to interfere when they did. "All right, Miz . . . "

"Pritchard."

"All right, Miz Pritchard. You fix up the papers you need for your laws, and I'll sign them."

"Good. Is Casey here, by the way?" I asked. "He missed the last class today, too."

"The junior varsity team's playing over at Naperville this afternoon," Tim said. "Casey ought to be home pretty soon now."

"Don't you have a record of when them boys are out playing ball?" Sam Jordan's voice indicated that he didn't think I was doing my job all that well. I was glad we were outside the circle of light so he couldn't see my face flush. Obviously Casey's last period teacher hadn't checked the daily bulletin, and I hadn't either.

"Yes we do. I missed it."

Jordan gave a little grunt, not particularly hostile, just indicating that that was about what he expected from women and schools. Tim seemed almost friendly by contrast. He walked me back to my car, and I felt the connection I'd been groping for. I knew where he was now, and it seemed a good place to be.

18

"Thanks for coming out," Tim said. "I know Dad's not easy to get ahold of." His glance ran over the Mercedes appreciatively as I got in, and I was particularly glad that it wasn't a beat-up Volkswagon as the engine turned over smoothly and I drove back down the long gravel lane to the road.

When I rounded the curve coming up to the bridge over the Feather River, the headlights swept an empty expanse of fenceline and roadside. Brandon wasn't there. I pulled off into the dirt road that ran along the river bank, turned off the lights, and rolled the window down. I shivered in the damp night air and decided to get my down jacket and hiking boots out of the trunk. I knew I wasn't going back to town without trying to find Brandon, and I knew I wasn't patient enough to sit there and wait, so I might as well be dressed for crashing around through the underbrush. It was full dark. No moon, or none that shone through the heavy overcast. I took the little flashlight from the glove compartment, put it in my jacket pocket, and started walking along the path that led under the bridge and toward the old cabins.

I'd gone maybe a hundred yards when I heard rustling in the bushes ahead, and suddenly Brandon hurtled into me, nearly knocking me over. He called out, throwing his arms up and trying to twist out of the hold I had on him to try to keep my balance.

"Brandon! Calm down! What's the matter with you?"

"Mrs. Pritchard?" He grabbed me, taking handfuls of jacket and holding on.

"OK, OK, everything's all right. Just calm down." I put my arms around him, then loosened his grip and put the jacket around him, folding him inside it until he stopped shaking. "Come on, let's get back to the car."

He shook his head and moved away from me. "Mrs. Pritchard, there's a body back there in the path."

"Are you sure?"

19

"It's not the sort of thing I could easily be mistaken about."

"Is it Felipe?"

"I'm not sure, but I don't think so. Felipe's small. This felt like a man. But I couldn't see. Whoever it is is dead, but I don't think he's been dead very long."

"How far is it from here?"

"I'm not sure. I just started running. Not very far, I don't think. Maybe we had better go to the car. We better tell the police."

I thought about it. I didn't like it out in the dark any better than Brandon did, but I had my doubts whether the police would listen to Brandon if I weren't able to corroborate his story. "Brandon, remember when you told the police there was a cougar up on the ridge? And when you told them Julie Carter was being held for ransom out by the cannery buildings?"

"They're not going to believe me, are they?"

"If there's a body out there, you better show me where it is."

We started back along the path, the thin beam of my pocket flash picking out the narrow opening between the riverbank weeds that pressed in on either side. In places the path dipped down through marshy areas where the mud sucked at our feet, once pulling Brandon's tennis shoe off so he had to balance precariously while I retrieved it. We had gone what seemed like at least half a mile when the doubt in my mind reached an intensity strong enough to stop me.

"Brandon . . . "

"I wish I was making it up."

"Maybe you really thought there was a body, but it was so dark you were mistaken. Maybe it was an old pillow or something from one of the shacks."

"It's a body."

I had turned toward Brandon as I spoke to him, so I

20

saw his hand pointing before I saw the yellow-and-black checked lump in the narrow shaft of light. I knew that jacket; I'd seen only one like it— a lumberjack check, but yellow-and-black instead of the familiar red-and-black pattern—so I knew before I saw the freckles stark against the gray-white skin that it was Casey Jordan. His body lay jackknifed on its side, hands clutching the chest, a surprised rather than frightened look on his face, as though he couldn't figure out where all the blood had come from. The front of his clothing was the single solid brown of dried blood.

"It's Casey," Brandon said.

It seemed like I stood there for a long time. I don't know how long it actually was. It seemed like I thought very slowly about things, watching the ideas and images in my mind as though they were a movie. I watched Casey not be dead, saw him turn off the path into the gravel lane past the abandoned cabins, walk toward his house, into the circle of light where the men stood around the pickup. Saw his dad look at him and nod his silent greeting. Heard Tim ask who had won the basketball game. Then I saw another body lying in almost the same position. Rick. Bent over more. Twisted a little. The blood that soaked the front of his white lab coat and tan cords still bright red. Bright red against the white tile floor, bright red on the gurney he'd fallen against. So much blood.

"Mrs. Pritchard?" Brandon took the flashlight out of my hand. "Come on, we've got to go back to the car." He tugged at my arm and the beam of light moved erratically. We both saw the knife at the same time. Brandon stepped over Casey's body to go toward it.

"Don't touch it, Brandon."

"I know. I just want to see it." He bent over, the knife centered in the small circle of light. It was a switchblade. "It's Felipe's knife."

"Don't touch it."

"You said that already. Come on, let's get out of here."

Brandon went first with the flashlight, holding the sleeve of my jacket with his other hand. Neither of us wanted to lose physical contact, even when we came to the marshy places where the footing was tricky.

Then we were sitting in the car, looking out through the window at the indistinct shapes of trees, the black expanse of river current, the slightly lighter emptiness of cloud cover. I made no move to start the car. There seemed to be a lot that I should think about, but I didn't know what it was.

"Could we play the music? I mean without starting the car?

I nodded and put the key in the ignition. Brandon found the tape by touch, remembering where it fit into the carrying case, and slipped it into the playing deck. I wondered briefly if that were an odd thing for us to do, but it didn't seem to be. Right then it seemed like the immense sanity of Bach's music was what we needed more than anything else. We needed to know that a human being did that, too. When the second side of the tape had finished playing, we were able to talk.

Brandon said the things that had to be said that were easier when he said them. I wondered how he had the energy for that gallantry.

"I'm not in a very good position," he said. "I have some kind of reputation for being a delinquent. And I was down there alone at about the time someone killed Casey."

I nodded. "But you didn't touch the knife?"

"No. I only saw it when you did."

Brandon told me that he'd cut through the orchard on his way down to the shacks, so he didn't know if Casey's body was already there then. As he got closer he heard the sound of an engine, like some large type of machinery, or a plane taking off. He thought it was a plane, but it was too close, and there was no place for a plane to land or take off down there. But there was no large machinery, either. Just the engine sound. He'd checked the few cabins that were open, and found one that he thought had been used recently. There were fast-food containers and old blankets, but no indication of who had been there. By that time it had gotten dark. He lit one of the candles in the shack while he looked around, but when he went outside it kept blowing out in the wind. Since the area was obviously deserted, he decided to come back when it was light and he could examine the cabin thoroughly. He was at the other end of the row of shacks, down by the river, so he took the path back. When he stumbled over Casey's body in the dark, he took enough time to check for a pulse, found none, and started running.

"I probably have blood stains on me somewhere," he concluded. "There was an awful lot of blood. I felt it on his hand. He can't have been dead long because he wasn't stiff. And the blood was sticky."

I told Brandon briefly about my visit with Sam and Tim Jordan. We sat silent for a while, thinking of them. Thinking that they didn't know, were maybe wondering what was keeping Casey, but weren't even worried yet. They had maybe an hour or two of their old reality left before the new one broke in upon them.

"OK, we'd better go now. Anything else we need to talk about?"

Brandon thought for a moment, shook his head, then said, "Only . . . only about Felipe's knife."

"What about it?"

"Well, of course I don't think Felipe would kill anybody. I don't even think he'd hurt anybody if he could help it. But he's my best friend, so naturally I don't think

23

he'd do anything like that. He's been gone for two days. It doesn't seem logical that someone would be gone for two days, come back and kill a boy he hardly even knew, and then disappear again, right?''

"What are you getting at?"

"Well, he's gone. But his family hasn't told the police or anyone like that because they're scared. They're in the country illegally. So there's no record of when Felipe disappeared, and it looks like he has a reason for running away. But it can't be the real reason.''

"I see what you mean. But it could be a reason for him not to come back. If he knew about it.''

"Right.''

"We've got to go now. You know that this is going to be . . . well, hard, don't you?''

"Right.''

It was harder than I had thought. It was a long night. Long and nasty. There was a muted tinge of excitement running through it, the slightly self-conscious edge of bad TV drama, as though people were enjoying the adrenalin, the release from the interminable boredom of their small town lives.

As soon as we got to the Fair Oaks police desk in the city hall, the officer on duty, Jimmie Brandt, called the Butte County sheriff, because the McGraw place was outside the city limits. Sheriff George Pratcher was a Broderick Crawford look-alike, and spoke exclusively in short, low-pitched commands to one of his deputies, who relayed them to Jimmie, who was manning the telephone. Brandon and I sat on a bench next to the wall, largely ignored, as they located the various persons and vehicles deemed necessary. The coroner, Dr. Lampson from Oroville, arrived about half an hour later, and the ambulance with two attendants shortly after that.

Pratcher had questioned Brandon and me briefly when he arrived, and didn't speak to us again until everyone

24

was assembled and ready to go. I said that I would drive, but the sheriff asked Brandon and me to ride out in his car. We sat in the back, looking through the heavy mesh that protected the lawmen from us, or through the windows of the doors that opened only from the outside. I didn't like it.

We were out by the bridge for over an hour. It seemed like everything was being filmed in slow motion for later playback at normal speed. There was lengthy conferring and checking of equipment before they started down the path. Bob Lampson had worked with Rick at the clinic, so I'd met him before. He was the only one who spoke with Brandon and me while the others milled around. When they finally started down the river path, Brandon went with them while I waited in the car. It started to rain.

Nearly an hour later, the ambulance attendants, with the white shrouded body of Casey Jordan on a stretcher, were the first ones back to the road. Dr. Lampson and Brandon were with them. The sheriff and his men remained behind while we took the body into Oroville. Brandon and I rode with Bob Lampson to his office, which was also the coroner's office when such an official location was required, and stayed in the waiting room while the doctor examined the body. When Bob Lampson came out he had a perplexed look.

"Casey was killed the same way Rick was, Carrie. Only one wound, but it penetrated the heart. When the knife came out he bled to death within seconds." He looked exhausted. Since Rick's death he was badly overworked, trying to take over most of the case load at the clinic in addition to his own practice and his duties as coroner. "Do you want someone to take you home, Carrie?" he asked. "I can't see any reason for you to go through any more of this."

"Of course I want to go home. We all do. What about Brandon?"

"The sheriff wants Brandon to stay."

"Then I'll stay awhile. Until I can take Brandon with me."

"You don't have to stay," Brandon said. "I'm OK."

"Brandon . . . "

"Right."

It must have been Jimmie Brandt who went out to the Jordan place, because he came into Lampson's office with Sam Jordan about half an hour after we got there. They walked through the waiting room and into the back, and in a few minutes Sam Jordan walked back through, the same man with a new reality to get used to. I knew that it wouldn't happen all at once; it was something you had to settle into gradually. At first, for a day or so, it seemed like you knew it, but then you started to forget sometimes. Like maybe he'd be working on a tractor motor, concentrating on the problem at hand, and then he'd think, "About time for Tim and Casey to be getting home." And then he'd remember. It would take a while for it to work into his life.

When Sheriff Pratcher and his men came back, we went over to his office. Bob Lampson offered again to take me home, and then he left. One of Pratcher's deputies was sent to get Virgil Henshaw, and a sleepy-looking court reporter showed up to take down the statement I dictated. When Virgil Henshaw came in he was sober, or nearly so, and frightened. He hunched down in the chair that Pratcher indicated, his eyes darting to Brandon, to the sheriff, then back to Brandon.

"What time did you last see your son today, Henshaw?" Pratcher asked him, and my mild dislike for the sheriff solidified into something stronger.

"Well, sir, I don't rightly know the exact time. I—"

"All right, Henshaw, let me put it this way. Did you see your son today?"

"I work out at the packing plant, Sheriff. You know that. I get back about the time the boy goes to school."

"When did you see Brandon last?"

"I got in this morning about seven-thirty. I reckon he was there then."

"Did you see him then?"

"Well, sir I . . . "

Pratcher turned away abruptly and spoke to a deputy. "Take Virgil back to the packing plant, and take this kid down to Juvenile Hall. I'm not going to spend all night on this, and I want this kid under supervision. Get him into juvenile custody."

"I'll take responsibility for Brandon, Sheriff," I said. "He's not going to run away."

Pratcher sighed the great world-weary sigh I'd been treated to before when I'd asked for assistance from his office. A sigh that communicated his importance and the lack of understanding he experienced from the lesser minds with which he was surrounded. "Miz Pritchard," he explained with elaborate patience, "I know you mean well, but I've got a murder on my hands here, not a case of some kid playing hooky. I'm going to have to make the decisions here. Now, I'd like to have Brandon here under a little closer supervision for a couple of days while I figure out just what happened out on the McGraw place tonight. And Virgil works nights, as you probably know."

Sheriff Pratcher was well aware that I knew, since I had already spoken with him about the situation Brandon lived with, as well as about several cases of probable child abuse that I was aware of in Fair Oaks. It was not an area that interested Sheriff Pratcher very much.

I turned to Brandon. "You say. I don't know what we can do, but I'll get MacKenzie down here and find out if you say so. I don't think they can take you to Juvenile Hall without some sort of charges."

Virgil Henshaw rallied a bit from his cowed submission. "That's right. You can't . . . "

"Shut up, Henshaw. Now, Miz Pritchard, I'm just trying to look out for the boy's best interests. Those are good people over at Juvenile. They'll get him some dry clothes and warm food. He's pretty well tired out, I should think." Pratcher put a ham-handed arm on Brandon's shoulder, and Brandon didn't even flinch.

"It's OK, Dad," Brandon said, "you just go back to work. I'll be OK."

"Sure. Yeah. Probably the best thing," Virgil Henshaw muttered, and followed the deputy out of the room.

For some reason this skinny fourteen-year-old kid, his clothes wet and his hair plastered down over his forehead, shivering uncontrollably from hours out in the cold and wet without even a jacket on, seemed to be in charge. Pratcher was aware of it, and it annoyed him.

"Really. You go on home," Brandon told me.

"Take Miz Pritchard to her car," Pratcher ordered, and another of his men moved to my side.

"All right, Brandon. I'll talk to you tomorrow. And MacKenzie will be there in the morning, for sure," I said.

It was after midnight before I submerged in the steamy luxury of a hot Opium bubblebath. At first I thought I'd fall asleep right in the water, but although my bones were aching with exhaustion, I couldn't find the off-switch for my mind. It wasn't just nerves. I could feel my mind trying to think about something, and then I realized what it was.

Casey Jordan's death was a new reality for me, too. It rearranged my interior world because a part of my reality had been the assumption that Rick had been killed by an addict looking for drugs, probably someone just passing through who happened to see the clinic sign and the light on late after Rick had finished putting a cast on Raul Velasquez's broken leg. Supposedly Rick hadn't locked the door after the Velasquez family left, and the killer had slipped in, demanded drugs, and pulled a knife when Rick refused. This was the theory that Sheriff Pratcher had been satisfied with, and that I had accepted. No one had been seen near the clinic between the time the Velasquez family left and the time I got there and found Rick dead.

Now things looked different. Another person killed the same way: a knife that penetrated the heart so fast and accurately that the victim seemed not even to realize it, pulled the knife out with his own hands, and stared with astonishment at his own blood pumping out with the last strong contractions of the heart, leaving the body completely emptied. The door that I'd shut on Rick's death, thinking that I knew what had happened, wasn't shut anymore.

I didn't have any answers, but at least I had the question figured out. When I got into bed, I fell asleep immediately.

3

WHEN THE RINGING woke me I fumbled for the alarm button, but the noise didn't stop. I gradually achieved enough consciousness to realize that it was the telephone and not the clock.

"Carrie? This is Don. I woke you, didn't I? I'm sorry."

"That's OK. The alarm would have gone off in five minutes anyway." The clock read five to seven.

"I guess it sounds odd to wake you up to tell you to go back to sleep, but that's what I'm doing. You've had a rough time. I want you to take the day off and get some rest."

"I can come to work, Don. I'm all right."

"No, Carrie. Maybe if it were going to be an ordinary day, but it's not. You'd just have to answer questions all day. Frankly, I think the school routine will have a better chance of settling down if you take the day off, so I'm not being noble. I'll see you tomorrow."

So instead of going to work I went over to Mack's.

Mack had to be nearly seventy, and he looked it. He was carrying at least fifty pounds of weight that he shouldn't be, smoked too much and had the nicotine stained fingers and deep wracking cough that went with the habit. But his infirmities were only of the flesh, unless a curmudgeonly idealism is an infirmity.

Mackenzie had been a civil liberties lawyer for almost half a century, starting long before it was fashionable by defending Japanese-Americans who were deprived of their property and sent to detention camps during the Second World War.

Mack rode with me to Juvenile Hall, a long low adobe building of California institutional design that occupied an entire city block. Brandon was brought to one of the interview rooms. He had been thoroughly admitted: regulation haircut, pajamalike uniform, and a faint whiff of disinfectant about him.

"So far so good," he said. "I've been able to infiltrate so completely that no one suspects I'm not actually an inmate here."

"Brandon, you are actually an inmate here," I said.

"Right. So far so good."

Mack left to check the details of Brandon's admission, and I asked Brandon to be patient in case the red tape took a while.

"But I've got to find Felipe," Brandon said. "He may be in bad trouble."

"You don't exactly have the world by the tail yourself."

"That's true, but as everyone keeps saying, these are good folks. And it looks like Felipe may be with someone who kills people."

"Look," I said, "I have the impression that you don't think too highly of the adult members of your community, but at least let Mack take his best shot before you start concocting any of your harebrained schemes."

I got no promise from Brandon, and on our way back to Fair Oaks Mack told me that things didn't look good. He'd called Virgil Henshaw from the admissions desk. Pratcher had already talked to Brandon's father that morning and convinced him that protective custody at Juvenile was the best place for Brandon.

"It's damned hard to get a juvenile away from the law when they decide to protect him," Mack said. "Anything I could do has to be on behalf of Brandon's father. He'll

31

have to sign a release petition. Juvenile Hall probably *is* the best place for Brandon right now.''

"Sheriff Pratcher thinks it's the best place for him. You think it's the best place for him. And maybe it is, but Brandon doesn't think so. Doesn't he have any rights?''

"Hardly any.''

"Mack," I said when we were back in front of his place, "I need your advice.''

"You going to pay me? I don't care whether people take my advice or not, as long as they pay me.''

"What should I do about this business with Brandon? He's a good kid, really. And he's getting a bad deal. His father's an alcoholic, the school's trying to expel him, and now the sheriff's got him in Juvenile Hall, which will be on his record.''

"What should you do?" he asked. "What do you want?''

"I don't know," I said. "I'm not sure.''

"If you don't know what you want," he said, starting to get out of the car, "your chances of getting it are very slight.''

"Mack, wait a minute. I'm going to pay you whatever the going rate for sarcastic old grumps may be. I picked you up at eight-thirty, so start timing from then.''

"What does Brandon want, then?" he asked.

"Brandon wants to find his friend, Felipe Ramos.''

"He's a friend of the Ramos boy?" Mack showed a little interest.

"Yes," I said, "do you know Felipe?''

"No. I know his father, though. They want me to help them get residence permits and working papers so they can stay in this country legally.''

"You've been able to help quite a few of the families at the camp with that, haven't you?''

"They all want to become citizens so they can vote to keep the Cubans and Central Americans out," he said.

"Rick said that you were the only person he knew that really believed all humans were equal—equally rotten," I told him.

"Ramos called me Tuesday afternoon and told me his boy was missing. Wanted to know what he could do. I told him he should go to the police, and he asked if the police would ask to see his papers. I said they probably would."

"Maybe Felipe was picked up by an immigration patrol," I said.

"There weren't any in the area," Mack said. "I thought of that. Brandon has a rather inventive imagination, hasn't he? Isn't he the kid that had the National Guard out a few years ago? Making animal noises up on the ridge?"

"That was a long time ago. He was a lot younger and he didn't think people would overreact like that," I said. "I thought about that, too, when he started this business about Felipe. I thought it might be some foolishness the two of them thought up. But Brandon didn't invent Casey Jordan's death."

"So we're back to the question of what you want," Mack said. "After you know that, I can give you legal advice, whether it's going to help you or get in your way. Just because you know what you want doesn't mean you can get it. Or maybe you can get it, but you can't get it legally, in which case you don't want a lawyer. You may want one later, however."

"You think I'm a real featherhead, don't you?" I said. "Rick told me that you said he shouldn't marry me."

"He didn't pay me or take my advice," Mack said. "He did say that the way you organized the office and the bookkeeping made it possible for the clinic to make enough to keep going."

"Thanks for telling me that, Mack. I'm glad to know
. . . that Rick . . . ''

Mack started to cough, and then lumbered out of the
car and up his front walk, giving a parting wave over his
shoulder.

I started the car without even knowing where I was
driving to, which caused me to think about Mack's
advice—it was hard to act if you hadn't decided what it
was you wanted. Well, I knew what I wanted to do, there
was no doubt at all about that. But that was three months
away, and right then I didn't know which way to turn
when I got to the street corner.

It was a bright March day after the night's rain. A
beautiful day. When I turned right at the corner, it was
because I was heading for the river. At least it seemed
more reasonable to be heading out to the country on a
beautiful day than it would have in a storm. But that was
a fine point since going out there at all seemed decidedly
unreasonable.

I didn't leave the car by the bridge but drove into the
McGraw Orchards. It was a longer walk to the cabins
that way, but I didn't want to leave the Mercedes by the
road where it would be recognized by anyone who happened to drive by, and I also didn't want to walk along
the path and pass the place where Casey's body had
been. I wasn't sure why I was going to the cabins. For
some reason Brandon had thought that something down
there might help him figure out what had happened to
Felipe.

I left the car pulled to the side of the gravel lane, not
trusting the dirt service roads which had turned to mud
in the spring rains. When I got to the cabins, it was
apparent that the police had searched the area. Prints of
heavy boots trailed from one cabin to the next, and
seemed to concentrate around the second one from the
end, the one Brandon had thought was being used.

34

The cabin was one of the few that were not locked up, probably because the door was missing and it would have been more trouble than it was worth to board it up just to protect the few rickety pieces of furniture inside. There was an iron bed frame with a rusting bedspring over which a ragged and stained bed pad lay. Next to the head of the bed, directly across from the door, was a three-drawer chest with only the bottom drawer in it, empty except for an old newspaper used to line it. A stovepipe lay on the floor by the wall to the right of the door, and there was charred wood on the asbestos pad where a stove had once stood. A wooden table was in the center of the room, square with dirty plastic adhesive covering glued to the top. One kitchen chair, the kind made of tubular metal with plastic upholstered seat and back, sat by the table; another, this one wooden with a leg missing, lay on its side in the far corner.

The blankets Brandon had mentioned, two olive green wool ones that looked like military issue, were flung over one of the rafters above the bed, and there was a takeout box from Round Table Pizza and some Slurpee cups on the floor. It didn't seem like there could be anything that would indicate who had used the cabin. And if there had been, surely the police would have found it already. It was a nasty place, smelling of urine, and I had no inclination to stay and poke around. But if Brandon had been there, that's exactly what he would have done. I thought I could at least take him the assurance that there was absolutely nothing to indicate that Felipe had been there.

There wasn't a whole lot to poke at, anyway. I picked up the foul-smelling quilted pad from the bed and looked at the springs. I took the torn newspaper out of the lone drawer and looked at it and under it. There was a small shelf to the right of where the stovepipe no longer vented. On it were a box containing five wooden matches, three burned and two unused, and two candle stubs. There were cobwebs in all the corners and at the roof peak and along the support rafters. I stood on the one solid chair and checked that nothing had been hidden on the rafters. I took the blankets down and inspected them. And I felt silly, a supposed grown-up playing a fourteen-year-old's detective game.

It occurred to me that the police had no doubt looked in all of the places I had been looking in, and would know if things weren't left the way I had found them, so I tried to remember exactly the way the blankets had been hanging and the bed pad had been spread over the springs. The second time I climbed up on the chair, one of the legs went through a rotted floorboard and I lost my balance, knocking the chair over as I jumped down. The wood floor had splintered, leaving a hole that obviously hadn't been there before. The chair lay on its side, a big wad of pink bubblegum stuck to the inside edge of the metal tubing that supported the seat.

Bubblegum. I had a sudden mental image of Felipe, intent upon the controls of a video game, apparently oblivious to the large pink balloon shape issuing from his pursed lips. Bubblegum.

I went outside and broke a twig from one of the bushes, took it back into the cabin, and pried the hardened lump of gum from the bottom of the chair. With it came a shiny metallic oval that had been stuck on the inner surface. I quickly wrapped a tissue around the whole wad and thrust it into my pocket. I set the chair on its feet, not trying to put it back where I had found it since the hole in the floor made it obvious that someone had been in the cabin. It belatedly occurred to me that my fingerprints were all over every surface should anyone be curious about who had been there.

I hurried back through the orchard, down the long corridor formed by the overlapping branches of peach trees. My heart was racing and what felt like at least a pint of adrenalin was loose in my blood. All I wanted was to get away from there, get the Mercedes, which I wished was an anonymous beat-up VW, and get safely home. Miraculously, or so it seemed to me, I saw no one.

At home I double-locked the door and put the safety chain on. I made a pot of tea, and then a peanut butter and banana sandwich for lunch. When I finished eating I sat at the kitchen table and thought for a while. Things were happening too fast. If I didn't know what I wanted, my chances of getting it were very slight. Damn Mac. Damn Pratcher. Damn Rick for getting himself killed and damn Pratcher for not doing something about it. The only person who I knew was determined to find out what had happened out on the McGraw place was Brandon, because he wanted to find Felipe. And wherever Felipe was, he was probably with Casey's killer. And whoever killed Casey looked to be the same person who had killed Rick. Okay, Brandon, I thought, let's find Felipe. By the time I washed the few dishes I had used and put them away, I was ready to get the wad of gum out of my jacket pocket and inspect the object that had been stuck to it. Whatever it turned out to be, my decisions had all been made.

The silver oval was a cheap locket. On the front was the image of Our Lady of Guadalupe. When I opened the locket a small folded piece of newsprint fell out. On the paper four letters had been scratched in block capitals with a charcoal tip: I,S,L,A. The picture in the locket was so small that the faces of the three women could not be clearly seen, but they were Mexican. One wore a black shawl. The one in front seemed very young, only a girl. I folded the scrap of paper again and put it back inside the locket, and I put the locket, minus the bubble-gum, back into my jacket pocket.

All things considered, and there wasn't that much, it seemed likely that Brandon's hunch about Felipe being in that cabin had been right. That needed verifying, so I drove back to Juvenile Hall.

A rather surly attendant escorted Brandon to the interview room, where I was waiting for him—the official visiting time was on Friday evening, and I had to do some prevailing to convince the matron to let me talk to him.

"Brandon," I said, "no jokes, please. I need to know more about Felipe."

He looked at me appraisingly, and I realized how far our little bantering game was from being trust. I was looking at a boy who had developed several ingenuous masks to protect himself from an erratic world of adults, but who had no connection with that world. "Why?" he asked, and I knew he meant both why did I want to know and why should he tell me.

"I want to find Felipe because there may be some connection between his disappearance and my husband's murder. I found something that may be Felipe's."

"What?"

"You first. Tell me about Felipe. What part of Mexico he came from, how you happened to become friends, why he had a knife like that, what kind of person he is. Just tell me about him."

"How do I know you really have something? Where did you find it?"

"I found it out at the cabin you told me about, and if you can't trust me that much—that I wouldn't flat out lie to you—then I don't think there's any sense in talking." I got up from the cracked naugahyde sofa we were sitting on. I was a bit shaken by what I saw behind our jokes—there wasn't much, but at least enough that when I'd said, "no jokes," he hadn't given me any.

"If you've found something, why don't you give it to the police?"

"Because I don't think it would mean anything to them, and it might to you. But that's it, Brandon. I'm not going to show you unless I get some cooperation from you."

He thought about that for a moment, and then started talking. "I met Felipe about a year ago. Not quite a year. School was nearly out for the summer. The first time I saw him was at the 7-11. I was playing the video games. It was in the morning so I was the only one in there."

"You mean everyone else was in school?"

He nodded. "That was before they started not letting anyone under eighteen play the games during school hours. I suppose that was one of your ideas."

"Not my worst one, either."

"Felipe came in by himself and stood behind me and watched. I'd won a couple of games, about five or six probably—I usually do—and it was getting boring, so I asked him if he wanted to play. He just looked blank, so I asked him in Spanish and he said he didn't know how. He did of course. He was trying to set me up."

"You mean to bet on a game?"

"Sure. But I expected that, and I didn't think he'd be as good as I was. While he was watching I wasn't playing as good as I can."

"Kindred souls."

"Right. We are. He's my friend."

"How old is Felipe?"

"A few months older than I am. He's fifteen."

"And what, besides a predilection for hustling video games, do you find to like about Felipe?"

"Well, he's clever. I mean he's funny, and he thinks of interesting things to do. He pretends he can't speak or understand English and—"

"But he does speak English?"

"Sure. But he gets away with a lot by pretending he doesn't."

"So far all the things you've told me are about taking advantage of people, or misleading them. I can't say that I find that very attractive," I said.

"You didn't ask me about what you would find attractive."

"Right. What about the knife? Do you find carrying a deadly weapon attractive?"

"Not particularly."

"So?" I asked. "What do you think about Felipe carrying a knife?"

"I think it's like wearing a bone in your nose."

"What do you mean?"

"If I wore a bone in my nose in Fair Oaks," Brandon said, "it would be very odd. But if I lived in Africa in a tribe that did that, and wore a bone in my nose, it would just be normal."

"I've been to Mexico, Brandon," I said. "Quite a few times. I don't believe that it's any more normal for Mexicans to carry weapons than it is for North Americans."

"It's normal for Mexicans here."

"Why?"

"Why would anyone put a bone in his nose? Also, Felipe was good with it. Like people practice target shooting with a rifle. That doesn't mean they're going to shoot somebody."

"Was he good enough to kill someone if he wanted to?"

"I think so. I am, too. Do you think I could have killed Casey? I was down there when it happened. I could have had Felipe's knife."

I thought about it, really trying to believe that Brandon could have stabbed Casey, but I couldn't. I shook my head. "No, I don't think you could have."

"Why not?"

"I really don't know. It's mainly just a feeling about you."

"Well, you don't know Felipe, but I know him a whole lot better than you know me."

"What else do you know about him?"

"If he says he's going to do something, and he's serious about it, then he'll keep his promise. He works hard, harder than most people do picking or pruning. I go with him sometimes. Sometimes I stay at his house."

"Where do they come from in Mexico?"

"They used to live in a village near Morelia. That's between Mexico City and Guadalajara. It's right on a lake. Cuitzeo it's called, and that's the name of the lake, too. His mother is still there with the little kids. That's why he works so hard, so they can come here, too."

I took the locket out of my pocket. "Do you recognize this?"

"It looks like Felipe's. He had one like that that he wore on a chain around his neck."

"If it's Felipe's, what did he have in it?"

"A picture of his mother and sister and grandmother. He called them his women. He misses them a lot."

I handed Brandon the locket, and he opened it. He opened the little piece of paper and looked at it. "What's this?"

"I don't know. I thought maybe you'd know. I thought maybe you and Felipe might have had some kind of code you used."

He shook his head. "We never needed one. If we were around Anglos, we spoke Spanish, and if we were around Mexicans, we spoke English. If someone spoke both we used pig Latin."

"Pig Latin? Are kids still using pig Latin?"

"Just me and Felipe that I know of."

"Erewhay idday ouyay earnlay igpay atLayinay?

"Elayoay enay unay ilayobray."

"Spanish too. Should cover most situations."

"*Isla* is the Spanish word for island," Brandon said. "But what island? This doesn't make any sense. Where did you find it?"

I told him about my visit to the cabin.

"Are you going to give this to the sheriff?" he asked me.

"No. I brought it to you. I didn't know if it was Felipe's, and now that I know that, I still don't have any idea what it means. I thought you would."

"I don't, though."

"Brandon?"

"I really don't."

I realized that whether he did and wasn't telling me, or whether he really didn't, there was nothing I could do. I'd made my decisions; there was no sense in thinking about them anymore.

"I'll come by tomorrow evening. Is there anything you want me to bring you?"

"How about release forms?"

"How about a Snickers bar?"

"No thanks, bad for my teeth. I don't need anything."

As I drove back to Fair Oaks, I glanced at the time: just twenty-four hours since I had been looking for Brandon. At least today I knew where to find him.

4

THE SHOCK WAVE caused by Casey's death had spent its first force on Fair Oaks High the previous day, but there were strong tremors when students saw me in the halls, knowing I had been out there when it happened. Don had been right about the disruption. I had a few home calls to make, so it seemed a good day to be away from the campus. I stopped by the administration office to tell the secretary I'd be back in time to send out call slips for detention, and while I was there I picked up the work-study application for Tim Jordan. I wanted to have it ready when he came back. If he came back.

The home calls, as usual, provided glimpses into worlds of stupefying, apathetic misery. A thirteen-year-old girl left to care for a sick infant and twin three-year-old brothers by a mother she hadn't seen for two days. An obese boy so tormented by his classmates that he would sneak back home after his parents went to work, to watch TV and eat junk food all day. Another girl, pregnant and unmarried, who had been thrown out by her father and unwillingly taken in by a married sister, also pregnant, who lived with her unemployed husband and two children on the second floor of a shabby residence motel. As I left this last place I picked up a tiny plastic giraffe, the kind of toy that comes in cereal boxes, and sat down on the open wooden stairs holding it in the palm of my hand. I thought about the next name on my list, knew the situation there wasn't going to be any better, and decided to stop by the McGraw house first.

The McGraws lived on the corner of Kentucky and Walnut. In Fair Oaks the streets running north and south are named for states and the streets running east and west are named for trees. Walnut Street had been the most elegant street in town at the turn of the century, and still was. The Victorian houses, kept up or restored by the few wealthy families left, presided over their deep lawns and bountiful rose bushes with a graciousness not achieved by even the most expensive of the newer houses on Maple Street or Pine Street.

On Walnut Street it seemed a blessing that the flow of time and prosperity had passed Fair Oaks by, that being on the railroad line no longer meant civic growth, that the new highway that might have brought in new business ran by ten miles to the east, that the old downtown area contained as many boarded-up storefronts as it did operating businesses. On Walnut Street it seemed that the past glory had achieved a patina that made it all the more desirable for being past and untouched by the vulgarity of modern wealth.

Crocuses were blooming and thick blunt tips of hyacinths were nudging through the narrow beds of rich earth that bordered the broad walk to the McGraw house. The house had belonged to Harriet's parents, as had most of the acreage that was now included in the McGraw Orchards. When the old couple had died, Jensen and Harriet had moved to town and Harriet had spent a small fortune restoring the place. When she greeted me at the door with her wonderful smile, I could hardly blame Jensen for wanting to please his wife.

"Carrie! What a lovely surprise. Come in, please come in."

I was aware that I hadn't really thought that Jensen McGraw would be there—I was just glad of an excuse to visit Harriet. The room we were in was one of the most beautiful I'd ever seen, with brilliant Turkish rugs, deep wine velvet sofas piled with cushions, a civilized jungle of palms and ferns, and several pre-Columbian art objects that would drive a museum director mad with covetousness.

"Is Jensen home, by any chance?" I asked.

"No, he's in Sacramento. But how lucky, you're just in time for lunch, so you didn't waste a trip at all. What do you want with Jensen?"

"I really just wanted an excuse to come for lunch," I said, "but I was also hoping that he could sign a work-study form for Tim Jordan."

"Well, tell me about it, and I can have Jensen sign it tonight, unless there's more to it than a signature."

I was following her as we spoke, through the room that would have been an everyday parlor in Victorian times, through the library lined with floor-to-ceiling glass-fronted book shelves, and into the solarium which was Harriet's studio. She sculpted ornamental bronzes for fountains and was currently working on a clay model.

"Oh, Harriet! Harriet that's marvelous."

She looked as delighted as the three little clay children she had created. Her sculpture was so convincing that I could see and hear the water they would be playing in, one child holding a garden hose from which would come a stream of water that another would deflect with out-stretched hands while a third sat in the pool, playing with a boat that would float on the water's surface.

"Aren't they having a good time? I saw them last summer, just like that," Harriet said. "Or that's the way I remember them. They were playing in a wading pool in a yard on Virginia Street."

"And where are they going?" I asked.

"To an estate in Marin County. If my client likes it, that is."

"How could anyone resist them?"

"I hope the client is pleased. I really am quite excited

45

about this one. I'll show him the model this week, and then I can get started." Harriet smoothed a piece of clay to accentuate the apple-cheeked smile of the child holding the hose. She seemed engrossed in and enchanted by her work—it was as though she was watching something amazing happening, independent of any activity on her part. Maybe it was like that, her eyes and hands taken over by a process, the creation of wonderful children who grew from clay and bronze instead of flesh and bones.

Harriet was in her fifties, at a distance indistinguishable in her lumpy outline from hundreds of other aging women, short and thick, with a close-cropped head of iron gray hair that didn't receive much attention. She had lived in Fair Oaks all of her life, as much as her life could be related to exterior accidents such as geographical location. Her family's wealth had been founded on original land grants, and Harriet's marriage to Jensen McGraw, who at that time was hardly more than a dirt farmer, had dismayed the community so much that more than thirty years later, many of the older residents still referred to her by her maiden name. Jensen's obvious devotion to his wife seemed his only creative attribute. Aside from that he was entirely a conservative community pillar, chairman of the school board, Rotary president, loyal chamber of commerce member. He'd married money, but he'd made a lot of it, too.

"Excuse me," Harriet said, "I'll tell Rosa to fix our lunch now. Then you can tell me about the papers you have for Jensen."

Over delicious enchiladas I told Harriet briefly about Tim's wanting to work with his father during the afternoons, and a little about the program that would give him credits toward graduation. I couldn't tell whether she knew about Casey Jordan's death and chose not to mention it, or whether somehow she hadn't heard. Harriet had, sometime long before I met her, chosen the good, the true, and the beautiful, and without apology refused to give her attention to any of the other aspects of experience. Period.

"That's sensible," Harriet said. "Tim seems a serious young man. I remember he helped Jensen with the car one day when we were out there. I'm sure Jensen will be glad to have him working for the orchards. Now, Carrie, it's really fortunate that you stopped by today. I was just about to call you. You must come to the Yucatan with me over Easter, really. We've talked about it so often, and this is the perfect time."

"Oh, Harriet, I would like to. But I can't right now. I've got to use the time during the spring break to get the paperwork caught up at the clinic or we'll never find a doctor to take over. I *am* going to go with you some time. Maybe next year."

"You have been saying that for three years now. If you would just once see how beautiful it is . . . It really would be a favor to me, Carrie. Jensen can't get away, and it's so much more fun to have someone to share it with. The beaches are so marvelous, and we'll drive down to Tulum . . . "

"But tell me about this," I said, indicating a figure in the window bay of the dining room. "It's beautiful. I'm sure I haven't seen it before."

Harriet nodded. "Mayan. The mosaic is quite amazing, isn't it? Actually I'm thinking of using something similar—not jade of course, maybe ceramic tile—for a commission I have for a figure for a little garden pond."

She went on describing her idea, and as usual I could see the images she was describing almost as though I were looking at a finished piece. In Harriet's world there was no dividing line between the visualized, the work in progress, and the completed form. Everything was process and energy.

47

"Harriet, I would like to stay forever. It's so beautiful here. But I have to get back to the high school. Thanks for a delicious lunch, and I'll stop by for the papers some time early next week."

She showed me out, with a hug at the door and an admonition to reconsider about going with her to Cancun, but I could tell by her abstracted expression that she was already playing with her clay children, even before the door had entirely closed behind me.

Back at the high school I found a note in my mailbox informing me that there would be an enrollment committee meeting at two o'clock in the conference room. That left me only forty-five minutes to get out detention reminders, so I winnowed through the list and called only those students I suspected of Friday afternoon skulduggery.

The enrollment committee consisted of two teachers, one of the guidance counselors, the vice-principal, the principal, and myself. Its function was not to enroll but to suspend or expel students. The purpose of this meeting was, as it had been frequently, "the Brandon Henshaw problem." The six of us sat around the oval table that the principal had chosen for his consensus procedures.

"Thanks for making time for this," Don said. "It may seem inappropriate to discuss this now, since Brandon is currently in Juvenile Hall, but we all know the problem has been blowing up for some time. I think it would be to Brandon's benefit to have this decision made before his release, so that he can get started immediately in whatever program seems most suitable."

"This is an academically talented kid, Don," Jim Herrero said. Jim was the Spanish teacher and one of Brandon's strongest partisans.

"Exactly what do you mean by 'academically talented'?'' the history teacher asked, giving Jim one of her stony looks. "He certainly has not displayed any talent in my class, on such rare occasions as he has attended. He pays no attention to the lesson but sits in the back and reads some trash or other."

"Sorry for the jargon," Jim said. "I mean Brandon's a bright kid. The last trash I caught him reading was *Les Misérables*, by the way, and I don't want to see him shunted into some program for losers, that's all."

The guidance counselor cleared his throat. "Perhaps it . . . ah . . . would be wise to consult all of Brandon's teachers to find if . . . ''

"You're Brandon's adviser," the principal said. "What's your appraisal of the situation?"

"Well, ah . . . I would say that Brandon . . . most of Brandon's teachers seem to feel . . . ''

"What is Brandon's schedule this term?" Don asked him.

"Ah . . . let me run down to my office for Brandon's card. I wasn't aware . . . ah . . . I didn't know that's what the committee meeting was about. I'll just be a minute."

I knew Brandon's schedule as well as I knew my own, but I was sitting this one out. Jim Herrero gave me a perplexed look, expecting my support. I gave him a smile instead.

"I would also like to say, Don," Jim said, switching his attention back to the principal, "that just because you began by saying that this is an inappropriate time to be discussing this doesn't make the fact that we *are* discussing it go away. Brandon Henshaw has enough problems right now. Why can't we table this until after he's released from Juvenile?"

Don nodded. The history teacher had no reaction. I smiled at Jim again. The counselor came back with Brandon's schedule.

"Jim was just saying," Don said, "that he thinks we should wait on this because there's a chance Brandon's attitudes may have changed as a result of this unfortunate experience."

"Brandon is not the only student involved," the history teacher said. "It isn't fair to the other students to have him popping in and out of classes whenever he feels like it. It's time he faced the consequences of his irresponsibility."

"Well . . . ah . . . yes," the counselor said, looking at the schedule, "but that sounds as though the Open School program were in some way punitive. It is not. That is . . . ah . . . I certainly think that it is not. It is designed to be academically valid, to lead to a high school diploma . . . but, ah . . . to also accommodate the nontraditional student."

"It is designed to get the nontraditional student, whatever that means, out of our hair," Jim said. "Have you been over there? Where do these kids go besides away? How many hours a week are they in class? Or with a tutor? Or whatever?"

"Well, ah . . . I don't have the statistics . . . ah . . . but it is an innovative and highly respected program."

And so it went. That far into the school year, each of us could probably have done all the voices by ourselves.

"Carrie?" Don asked after the others had repeated themselves about three times each. "You haven't had anything to say. You've spent quite a bit of time with Brandon. What is your feeling about the best way to proceed?"

"Well, we all know that Brandon's attendance record is not good," I said, "and that he receives almost no supervision at home. His test scores indicate he could probably do well in school if he attended regularly, but he does not."

Hugh, the vice-principal, spoke up. "You seemed to

be making some progress with Brandon, Carrie. I think that if you continued to work with him he'd probably settle down and do all right—''

Don broke in. "It seems that the consensus is that Brandon would be better off in the Open School, but I don't want to shut off discussion. If you wish, we can continue it next week, because our time's about up today.''

He wasn't quite quick enough. Don had thought I'd fight to give Brandon a chance to make his own decisions, but I hadn't taken the bait. And poor Hugh had blundered around and revealed the hook—it was bait to make me stay. The only thing I couldn't figure out was why Don was making such a big deal out of a simple thing like getting a new attendance monitor. It wasn't as if no one in Fair Oaks was looking for work.

"Well, Jim," Don said, "looks like it's up to you. Do we have a consensus to transfer Brandon to the Open School or shall we schedule another meeting for next week?''

"Consensus," Jim said.

He was leaning against the Mercedes when I got out to the staff lot after detention.

"Hi," I said, "what are you doing here this late on a Friday afternoon?''

"The good reason is that I was grading quizzes. The real reason is that I was waiting for you. Let's go have a beer.''

"My car or yours?''

"Are you kidding? Just riding in this Mercedes makes me feel intelligent," Jim said.

"OK, where to, then?''

We ended up in a booth at the pizza parlor with a pitcher of beer. Jim wanted to know what was up with me. I told him that Brandon truly did not give a damn about the Fair Oaks High School attendance policy, and, if the truth were told, I also, truly did not give a damn. About Brandon, yes, about his school attendance, no. At least not right then.

"From what I hear, you're not going to be here next year."

"Correct," I said. "But what I can't figure out is why Don Marquez is making such a fuss about my resignation. I don't think you were the only one who expected me to say that I thought Brandon should have another chance."

"You can't figure it out?" Jim said. "Well, I can. That worthless sonofabitch is so lazy that he has everyone else doing the work he should be doing. He doesn't want to lose you because you do all the work with the parents, which is his responsibility. He's probably on the make, besides."

"Tsk, tsk. Such disrespect for our leader," I said. "You applied for the position of principal when it was open, didn't you?"

"Carrie, you're a hard woman," Jim said, and then laughed. "OK. Yes. I applied for the position three years ago, and I would have done a better job than Marquez has."

"I don't know . . . "

"Thanks."

"No, let me finish," I said. "I think you're too good a teacher to be a good administrator. What does an administrator do? He administrates. He keeps things going without imposing his own ideas, finds out what the school board wants, what the parents want, what the teachers want. It seems to me Don is good at that. He just stays in the background and spreads a little oil around. You'd barge in and try to get everyone to do things your way. You get too involved in everything."

"Well, if not giving a damn is the only requirement for

52

a good principal, then we've got the best one in California. Probably in the whole country," Jim said. "Supposedly one of the most important qualifications for the position was being fluent in Spanish, being of Hispanic background. Equal opportunity and all that. So we hire someone who speaks Spanish. Does he go out to the labor camp to talk to the Mexican parents? No."

"But you do that, Jim," I said. "As long as the principal knows that things are being done, I don't see that he has to do everything himself."

"OK, OK," he said. "I guess Marquez isn't all bad. I'm just steamed right now because of this business about Brandon."

"Brandon certainly gets people stirred up, for some reason," I said. "I think the history teacher would have been glad to see him boiled in oil."

Jim grinned. "Brandon gets to you, all right. Let me say it before you do—one reason I like the kid so much is that he's one of the few students who really like studying languages. He's the only Anglo kid in the school who really speaks Spanish well, gets excited about it. He's started reading *Don Quixote*. It's slow going for him, but he plugs away at it. Likes it, too."

"I wonder how far he'll get, just doing things he likes," I said.

"I wonder, too," Jim said. "It sure runs against the grain of the Protestant work ethic, if nothing else. Brandon doesn't exactly have an easy life, though. There was a big flap about ten years ago—about a year or so after his mother died—her sister tried to get custody of him. Virgil was drinking pretty heavily, even back then."

"That's the aunt who lives in Sacramento?" I asked.

"Yes. Henshaw never forgave her. Won't even let Brandon visit her. She's about the closest thing he has to a possible stable influence in his life, and his father's got him cut off even from that."

"Well," I said, "it's a grim situation, but we can hardly say that it's beaten Brandon into cowed submission, broken his spirit, driven him to drugs and television serials."

"How about video games?" Jim asked.

"You win," I agreed, "his life is ruined. Which reminds me, I'm supposed to go over to Juvenile to see him."

After I dropped Jim off at the parking lot at school, I drove on into Oroville. It was nearly six o'clock, time for visiting hours at Juvenile Hall. There was quite a traffic flow of visiting relatives, so I wasn't surprised when I was asked to wait. But I was surprised when Sheriff Pratcher walked into the waiting room about ten minutes later.

"Are you here to see Brandon Henshaw, Miz Pritchard?" he asked.

"Yes," I said, "he skipped classes again today."

Pratcher was not amused by my little joke. "Brandon left here this afternoon," he said. "If you have any information or ideas about his whereabouts, I'd like to hear them."

"Left here? Without being released?"

"If you hear anything at all from or about Brandon, I want to know about it immediately. Is that clear?"

"Yes, of course. How did he leave?" I asked.

"Anything at all!" Pratcher said, and left the room.

5

GOING THROUGH THE clinic files was a job I'd put off for too long. There were odds and ends of paperwork—returned insurance claims, Medicare forms that had to be submitted again because of an error on the original—that had to be completed before the books could be closed on Rick's share in the clinic. Not that there was a line of hopeful practitioners jostling for position to buy into it, but the work had to be done just in case.

I went over there on Saturday morning. The clinic was busy, with the waiting room full of patients waiting to see the nurse practitioner, but I was in back with the files so I wasn't in the way. I needed to send one more notice to delinquent accounts before writing them off as uncollectable, so that was what I concentrated on first. I didn't expect that any of them would be paid. The people had not been inclined to pay a live doctor once they had recovered from whatever had ailed them, and they were less likely to pay a dead one. Still, it had to be done. The sooner all the loose ends were tied up, the sooner I could get on with my life.

It took me about two hours to work my way through the files. I was nearly finished when I took out the Velasquez file. As I opened it, an X ray slid out onto the floor, which was strange because the X rays were filed separately, not put into the patients' medical records and billing files. I picked it up and went out to the reception desk.

The receptionist, who also did the filing, said she

didn't know why the X ray was in there, but that she'd file it where it belonged on Monday when the clinic wasn't so busy if I'd just leave it where it was for now. I glanced at it as I went back to the file room, expecting to see a picture of Raul's broken shin bone, but the X ray was of someone's head.

I moved on to the delinquent W's and Y's, and then put the files away, took the billing information with me to work on at home, and gave in to my curiosity.

I didn't know that the sheriff would be in his office on a Saturday morning, but he was. As I walked in, he was calling through the open door, "Felicia, will you come in please?"

I didn't recognize Felicia, but I recognized her uniform from Juvenile Hall. I followed her into the sheriff's office.

"Is this about Brandon, Sheriff?" I asked. "If it is I'd like to hear about it. I'd like to know how he happened to leave Juvenile Hall without being released."

"Do you speak Spanish?" Pratcher asked me.

"A little."

"Do you speak English?" he asked Felicia.

"*Si, Señor,*" she said.

Pratcher sighed and motioned to his secretary, who was hovering behind me, to close the door. "All right, Felicia, now would you tell us what happened yesterday at Juvenile that ended up with Brandon Henshaw's leaving custody?"

Felicia was a plump, gentle looking woman in her late thirties, and she looked frightened.

"*No hay problema por usted,*" I said.

"Yeah," Pratcher said grudgingly, "*no hay problema. Por favor*, now, tell us what happened yesterday."

After this assurance that she wouldn't get into trouble by telling about Brandon, I asked her in Spanish how Brandon had managed to leave Juvenile Hall.

56

"*El muchacho* . . . the boy Brandon, he say Guadalajara *on playa* . . . *sur la mar* . . ."

"Brandon said Guadalajara was near the ocean?" I asked her.

"*Si,* near the ocean. I say no. I come from Guadalajara, close there in Nayarit. *No on playa.* Brandon say yes."

"Can you understand her if she tells you in Spanish?" Pratcher asked me, and I nodded. I told Felicia to tell me what had happened in Spanish, and didn't interrupt her until she had finished. I managed to hear her out with a straight face.

During the late afternoon recreation break, after the inmates had completed their cleaning chores, Felicia had been one of the supervisors in the game room. There had been five attendants in the room, three men and two women, because at five o'clock visiting hours would start and they needed all of the staff to escort inmates to the interview rooms and back. Brandon, evidently aware that more supervisors means less supervision, had taken the opportunity to start a conversation with Felicia by asking her if she had family in Mexico, where she had lived, and so forth.

When she said that she had come from Nayarit, from a small village near Guadalajara, Brandon told her that he had visited Guadalajara and thought the beach there to be the most beautiful he had ever seen. Felicia said that Guadalajara was not near the sea and therefore had no beach. Brandon insisted that Guadalajara was on the ocean and had a beautiful beach. Felicia said he must be thinking of Mazatlán or Acapulco, but Brandon insisted she was wrong, and bet her five dollars, which he showed her to prove he could pay up if he lost, that Guadalajara was on the west coast of Mexico. How he had happened to have five dollars she did not know.

Felicia, emphasizing her zeal for educating this ignorant boy rather than her interest in the money, told us that she had escorted Brandon, at his suggestion, to the library, where there were maps with which they could settle their bet. The library, it turned out, was two doors down the hall from the main entrance. They each took one of the big atlases from the atlas case. Felicia rested hers on the top of the case and Brandon put his on the table directly behind her. Brandon noticed that she was leafing through the volume to find the map of Mexico, and showed her how to use the index in the back. She mentioned that he pointed out several entries in the index, Guadalajara, Mexico, Mazatlán, to demonstrate that any of them would refer her to the proper page. She had obviously been intrigued by this introduction to scholarship.

She found the map of Mexico, traced with her finger the road between Guadalajara and the Pacific. She turned in triumph, to see only the atlas on the table behind her, the map of Mexico in that one marked by a five-dollar bill. Except for herself, the library was empty.

I asked her how it had happened that there was no one at the front desk at that time of afternoon. She said that there was always someone at the desk, and in fact that there had been two attendants on duty at the entrance when she ran out into the hallway to see where Brandon had gone. They had been talking to each other when she came up to ask if they had seen him. When they said no one had been near the desk, she assumed that he had gone the other direction, back to the recreation room. By the time she had looked everywhere inside of the facility and had accepted the conclusion that he was indeed not there, a good fifteen or twenty minutes had elapsed.

When Felicia had finished her account I relayed it to the sheriff, who had been sitting watching us as we talked, allowing a pencil to slip slowly between his thumb and index finger, eraser to tip, turning it over, tip to eraser, turning, eraser to tip.

"I don't see how he could have gotten far wearing one of those uniforms," I said.

"We had a report of clothing missing from a clothes-line in the east end," Pratcher said. "Jeans and a shirt. They belonged to a girl, but the way kids dress it doesn't make any difference. Ask her if Brandon said anything that might indicate where he was going."

I asked her and she shook her head.

"All right, Señora, you can go," he said. Felicia smiled a vague relieved smile, glanced from Pratcher to me and back, and fumbled her way out the door.

"And where do you think Brandon Henshaw has gone?" Pratcher asked me. It surprised me a little, and I realized that Pratcher knew he was in over his head. Whatever was going on in Butte County was as baffling to him as it was to me, despite his two terms as sheriff. Crimes of casual violence—robbery, rape, even mur-der—were not that uncommon. But whatever was going on didn't fall into any of the familiar sordid categories.

"I don't know," I said. "I don't see how he could go much of anywhere. All I know is that he wanted to find his friend Felipe."

"That's Felipe Ramos? The boy the knife belonged to?"

I nodded. "Did you talk to Felipe's father?"

"The night Casey Jordan was killed we went to the camp," Pratcher said. "Ramos said his son had been missing for two days. The next morning I sent a deputy down there to get a missing person report, and they were gone."

"Gone? Felipe's father was gone?"

"The whole family was gone. There was nothing in that house but the refrigerator and stove that belonged to the camp. Everything else was gone. The neighbors didn't know anything. Nobody ever knows anything down at the camp. This time not even the people who get paid for knowing knew anything." The pencil slid rhythmically through Pratcher's fingers.

"So what happens next?" I asked him.

"You see the posters all over every supermarket and drugstore? All the pictures of lost kids?" Pratcher asked me.

"Yes."

"It's not easy to find missing kids. People don't really look at kids. If you have any ideas about where Brandon might be, anything at all, I'd like to hear them."

"What could you do if he's gone to Mexico?"

"Jesus! Mexico? Why the hell would he go to Mexico?"

"I don't know. But I know that the last place he was seen was in the library in Juvenile Hall, looking at a map of Mexico. He might have had more purpose in that than just the bet with Felicia."

"How could a kid like that go to Mexico?"

"Brandon doesn't have . . . well, he doesn't have the same awareness of limitations that other fourteen-year-olds have. He's been knocking around on his own too long. If he wants to find Felipe, and if he thinks maybe Felipe is in Mexico, then he'll probably try to go there to find him."

"Where would he get the money? He couldn't walk from here. He couldn't hitch a ride without getting picked up by a patrol."

"I don't know," I said. "You said you wanted to hear any ideas I had, and that was the only idea I had."

Pratcher sighed. "Yeah. Well, if you hear anything from him, let me know. And don't get mixed up in anything else."

"We've got spring vacation coming up. I won't be

working after Wednesday. And I'll catch up on my paperwork until then."

"Fine," said Pratcher. "That's fine."

I did go in to talk to Jim Herrero before classes on Monday morning, though. He was the only person I knew who really had connections at the camp. He'd grown up there, and although there were some who thought he'd sold out because he was a teacher, there were plenty of others who were proud of him. He knew what went on at the camp, even though he didn't live there anymore. And what he didn't know he could usually find out since he had tutoring sessions out there several times a week for the workers who wanted to improve their English.

"I hear the Ramos family moved last week," I said. "Do you know where they are?"

"Not for sure. I know Señora Ramos has a cousin who lives out on the other side of Sutter Buttes. Her husband—the cousin's husband—has a job over there working for one of those big outfits growing sunflowers. They let them have an old farmhouse that was on the place. My guess is that Mack would know if anyone did. Antonio Ramos trusts him, and he's not supposed to move without notifying the court."

"That doesn't make any sense. If the court knows where he is, then Pratcher knows where he is, right?"

"Not exactly. The law moves in mysterious ways."

"It surely does. Explain, please."

"I just heard about this one because it's come up before," Jim said. "If an attorney is notified of his client's change of address, it qualifies as being notification to the court, since presumably the judge can contact the attorney. Of course the attorney is actually supposed to inform the court, but there's no time limit stipulated, and Mack tends to take a little time getting around to it. That's why he's got so many clients out at the camp."

"But the sheriff could get the information if he wanted it badly enough, couldn't he?"

"Sure. But it would take a while. There's no love lost between Pratcher and Mack. What you folks call a Mexican standoff."

I looked around Jim's classroom. I didn't have any response for his bitterness, but Rick had bought me exemption from it. I didn't particularly deserve it, but the widow inherits the deceased's estate. Even if it only amounts to accumulated good will.

Jim had colorful racks of comics and paperbacks, both English and Spanish, and cassettes of popular music and stories in both languages. He taught beginning and advanced Spanish classes, and filled out his schedule with English as a second language for migrant kids who didn't know enough English to be able to handle the regular classes. He structured his study units around Department of Motor Vehicle test manuals, want ads, state unemployment forms, and birth control pamphlets. His classes should have been called "Beginning Survival."

At the back of the room hung a big wall map of Mexico. I told Jim about Brandon's exit from Juvenile Hall, which made him laugh.

"Where do you suppose he is?" he asked.

"I really don't have the slightest idea. That's why I want to find out where the Ramos family is." I inspected the peninsula sticking out into the Caribbean Sea. "Have you ever been to Yucatan, Jim?"

"You may not believe this, but I've never been to Mexico," he said. "We could never afford the trip when I was young. After my grandparents died we had no close relations down there. Never got around to it, although I'm hoping to some day. Why? Are you planning on going to Yucatan?"

"Some day. Harriet McGraw invited me to go down there with her. They've got a condominium in Cancun, and she thinks it's the most beautiful place she's ever seen. I want to go, but . . . " I'd found Cancun on the map. It was on the eastern coast of the peninsula, directly east of Mérida. To the north of Cancun, a long slender island, probably an exposed extension of a barrier reef, followed the coastal contour. *Isla Mujeres*. Island of the Women. *He called them his women*, Brandon had said. Women. *Mujeres. Isla Mujeres*.

"But what?" Jim asked. "If the McGraws invited me, I wouldn't hesitate a minute."

Isla Mujeres.

"Oh, I just can't afford the time or the money. It does seem like a great opportunity, though, doesn't it? Maybe I should go. I don't really have any plans for spring break."

Isla Mujeres. It had to be. And Brandon had to have found it, too. Not by accident, but because that was what he had been looking for in the atlas index. *Isla Mujeres*.

"Maybe I'll tell Harriet I changed my mind," I said.

6

THE AIR WAS soft in Mérida, soft and thick and heavy, and everything moved through it slowly. We arrived in the afternoon during siesta, so the shops were shuttered, the streets nearly deserted except for an occasional very thin dog stretched out in the shade. We were staying the night, in a wonderful old hotel with massive Spanish furniture and slowly revolving ceiling fans, because Harriet wanted to do some shopping before we headed for the coast.

As the town came to life in the warm evening, we walked through the old part of the city to the cathedral square with its narrow streets leading off through the stone arches that had been the ancient gates of the city. Harriet was a good guide. She knew the history of the area, but preferred the visual present, was delighted with a brilliant cascade of bougainvillea over a stone wall or the shadows cast by a wrought iron gate onto the cobblestones.

We wandered into the labyrinth of the market, looking at the brightly embroidered white costumes the Indian women wore, short frocks over longer lace petticoats, the yokes of the dresses decorated with colorful flowers and birds.

In a side street leading away from the market area, Harriet steered me into a brightly lit shop that sold tourist trinkets, cheap ceramics and onyx chess sets, the Last Supper done in day-glo colors on black velvet, and plaster replicas of Indian artifacts. It hardly seemed

Harriet's style, but when the proprietor saw her come in, he moved immediately to the curtained doorway that led to a room behind the shop, and with a courtly gesture motioned us through.

"Señor Carillo's the agent for an artist who does marvelous reproductions," Harriet said to me. "You've seen some of his work at my house. *Buenes noches*, Señor Carillo."

"*Por favor*, sit here, Señora, Señorita," the man said, indicating two metal folding chairs by a wooden table. Harriet put on the little half-glasses she wore to inspect things closely, and he set several objects on the table one by one. The first three were figurines carved from a porous gray stone. They ranged from about four inches to a foot high. If they were reproductions, they were certainly convincing. And if they were reproductions, why weren't they displayed in the front of the shop?

Señor Carillo then took a burlap-wrapped bundle from one of the rough wooden shelves that lined the room, and carefully unwound the fabric. Inside was a pottery figure, a squat, complacent-looking Mayan matron with a small child in her arms and a snub-nosed dog at her feet. The figure wore a fez-shaped hat, large coiled earrings, and beads around her neck. Had she not been naked to the waist, one would not have been surprised to come upon her in a suburban street.

Harriet gave a little gasp of delight. "Wonderful." She turned the figure in her blunt capable hands. "Nearly perfect condition. Simply wonderful. Look, Carrie, how the little dog solves the problem of balance. She's a little pyramid." She handed the figure back to Carillo. "Yes, definitely. What else have you to show us?"

Another burlap bundle revealed a sculpted pottery jar with a surface that seemed to writhe with deep relief carvings. It stood about seven inches high and had obviously been broken. Animal forms, geometrically depicted, were a part of headdresses, or perhaps helmets and armor. Human faces in profile formed a part of the intricate design, faces with high-bridged aquiline noses, prominent cheekbones, and receding chins. "What a shame," Harriet said, running a finger over the badly chipped rim. "It's a magnificent piece, but in this condition . . . Well, I'm not sure. Let's see what Riano can do. Maybe he can make a mold from it."

Carillo nodded and rewrapped the jar. "I happen to have a piece you will enjoy," he said. "It is for a museum, of course, but they have entrusted it to me until the shipping is arranged. Perhaps Riano . . . " He pulled aside a drapery that hung before a closet and bent over an old metal safe from which he took a wooden box. He placed the box on the table and lifted off the lid, felt through the shredded newspapers inside, and carefully lifted out a jade mask. The face was smaller than life size, but with the headdress, ornately carved in stylized plumes, the piece was about ten inches tall.

Harriet took it almost reverently, turning it over to inspect the odd symbols on the curved inner surface. They were combinations of small geometric animal and human forms interspersed with irregular line designs, and combinations of dots and lines that reminded me of Morse code symbols. I moved my chair closer so I could see them better. "Glyphs," Harriet said. "Mayan picture writing. Probably similar to Egyptian hieroglyphics in being a combination of symbols for things and symbols for sounds in their language. But no one has ever figured out how to read them, unfortunately." She ran her fingers lovingly over the stone. "Yes," she said to Señor Carillo, "we must have Riano try a copy. Perhaps the green onyx . . . "

"Could I?" I asked. The surface of the jade made my fingers tingle with wanting to touch it. Harriet smiled and handed the mask to me. The surface was cool.

66

"Amazingly tactile, isn't it?" she said. "Something about jade makes you just have to touch it. And they'll put it behind glass in some museum. A shame."

The mask was nearly perfect. Only on the inner bottom edge, slightly off center to the left, had a small area been chipped away, defacing a part of the inscription, which no one could read anyway. I handed it back to Harriet, who gave it to Carillo. He replaced it in the safe and Harriet rose to go. "My husband couldn't come this trip. Perhaps he'll be down next month. I know he'll be interested in seeing what Riano is able to do."

"Harriet," I said when we were back on the street, "what a strange place. How does that man happen to have such things?"

"Ah," she said, "Señor Carillo is just a businessman. It's Riano you must meet. An artist with a feeling for the traditions of his people. He's Mayan. He makes very fine copies. His work is so respected that it's possible to convince the officials to bend the rules a little so he can have access to the finds to study and make sketches, sometimes to make casts, when that is possible."

"But where do these things come from?"

"From the earth, from the past, from the hands of artists," Harriet said. "More recently, I suppose, from Belize and Guatemala and Honduras, as well as from Quintana Roo and Campeche. Wait until tomorrow when we drive through Quintana Roo and you see the jungle. We'll stop at Chichèn Itza on our way. No one knows exactly how many similar sites there may be all through Central America, covered by jungle. Indian farmers sometimes find things when they clear land for a new field. Of course it would be better if excavations could be made, but where are these countries to get the money for such projects?"

We left Mérida early the next morning. Harriet smiled

when she saw me staring at the driver. "Do you recognize him?" she asked.

"Yes," I said. "Yes. It's amazing. I thought the carvings were stylized . . . I thought they were just designs. They're portraits."

"I don't know if they're actually portraits," Harriet said, "but they're certainly recognizable depictions of the Mayan Indians, aren't they? Mata might have stepped right off of one of the steles at Chichèn Itza."

We had lunch and spent two or three hours at the archaeological site. It was overwhelming. Little clusters of tourists huddled together reading guidebooks, as though the print could protect them from the strange power of the place. Harriet excused herself from climbing the steep narrow stairs that led to the jaguar throne inside the Temple of Kukulkan, claiming that she'd done it once and nearly succumbed to claustrophobia. I braved it, and saw the eerily beautiful figure in the chamber at the top, but I could definitely see what Harriet meant and was glad to get back down and out into the sunlight again.

"What are those odd little figures?" I asked Harriet, pointing to a statue that depicted a human figure lying on his back but with his head and knees raised. "You have one like that at your house."

She nodded. "There are literally hundreds of them. They're called Chac Mool, and seem to have some connection with ceremonies honoring the rain god. Maybe they're used as altars. No one really knows."

We continued east, driving through thick jungle. "You see why I'm so fascinated with Yucatan," Harriet said. "It's all mystery. Look, you can't see five feet into the jungle. It's a solid green wall. But everything it relinquishes is beautiful. The artifacts the Mayans left are priceless, although certainly collectors are paying prices for them—astronomical prices. Jensen said that the original mosaic piece that you saw a copy of in my dining room—remember it, the one you saw at lunch last week? The original brought over five hundred thousand dollars at an auction in New York.''

I nodded, although actually I found it all rather oppressive. There was a dense, closed feeling to the day—maybe from my long climb up inside the pyramid, or maybe that was only part of a larger pattern that included the thickly imaged carvings, the walls of jungle on either side of the road, the moist heavy heat. At any rate, it was a relief when suddenly we saw the sea.

"You would go that way to catch the ferry to Isla Mujeres," Harriet said, pointing to a road branching off the main highway. "There's an interesting Mayan observatory on the far side of the island, and a few good hotels at the north end, and good diving. Not much else. If you want to go over, I'll have Mata drive you to the ferry. I'm going to collapse on the beach tomorrow myself. I've really been working hard the last few weeks."

"I would like to see the island," I said. "Maybe I will go over tomorrow while you're sunning."

The condominiums and luxury hotels of Cancun loomed up ahead of us like a little piece of Southern California drifted loose from its moorings and come to shore on the Caribbean, expensive and familiar. The McGraws had the ninth floor of a glass-walled building set back from a long curve of white beach and calm cobalt water. Far out, the surf broke over a barrier reef.

Inside the decor was all chrome and Plexiglas and shiny plastic surfaces, as unlike the house in Fair Oaks as it was possible to imagine. "Keeps me from being homesick wherever I am," Harriet explained with an abrupt gesture around the living room. "Yucatan in California and California in Yucatan. I hope you don't mind my not going adventuring with you tomorrow. I really am beat. That commission—you remember the model I was working on? I finished it, but only just. Took it to be cast the day before yesterday. Barely had time to pack before it was time to rush for the plane.''

"Of course I don't mind. I like poking about on my own, really," I said. "If you don't mind my not lying around getting sand in my ears."

"Good. It's settled then. I'll check the ferry schedule, and Mata can take you any time you want to go in the morning.''

The ferry left the mainland at 10:00 A.M. It was a squat little tub whose engines emitted bluish brown diesel fumes, made a horrible racket, and shook the boat with teeth-rattling vibrations. Fortunately the crossing only took about twenty-five minutes.

I wandered around the little harbor town and studied the map in the tourist information office. The island was only a couple of miles across at its widest point, but over fifteen miles long. A road ran along the inner coast the entire length, but only occasional broken lines on the map indicated any access to the eastern side. At the northern end of the island there was open terrain, white sand and dune grass and magnificent tall coconut palms. The southern end seemed rather inhospitable, with a high ridge rearing out of dense tropical undergrowth.

Along the waterfront there were several little shops that rented snorkeling gear, windsurfing equipment, and motor scooters, so I was soon astride a battered Vespa heading north, feeling free in the heady way one does when alone in new surroundings. A causeway led across a wide marsh, and then a broad outcrop of rock supported a cluster of luxury hotels between the beaches on the east and west sides of the island.

I thought it likely that the trip to Isla Mujeres would turn out to be for no other purpose than the beautiful day, the sun-washed white sands, and the incredible blue of the Caribbean waters. It was difficult to think of any better reasons for being there.

I had seen Señor Ramos before I left Fair Oaks—with Mack's help I'd found the old farmhouse near Sutter Buttes—but I'd learned nothing. Well, almost nothing. Señor Ramos had come to the door when his sister-in-law's cousin had summoned him, but he hadn't really spoken to me. I was used to encountering that stolid mask when I tried to communicate with people in the camp who had no wish whatsoever to communicate with me. They spoke no English and did not acknowledge my Spanish.

But his complete lack of interest in my questions made me feel that he knew something. There was nothing that hinted of the anguish of a father whose son was lost. I asked him if he had seen Brandon Henshaw. He asked me, twice, who that was, went into the house, returned, and said no. I asked him if he had heard anything from Felipe. No. Beyond that his only comment had been, "*No hablo ingles.*" I knew that he did not speak English, but I wasn't speaking English, so his remark was something of a non sequitur. Whatever Señor Ramos did or did not know was not available to me. It probably had been available to Brandon, and Brandon almost certainly would have gone there. For that matter, he might have been in the house at the time I was talking to Señor Ramos.

Since my visit to Isla Mujeres was about ninety-nine percent tourist excursion, with only about one percent curious hope that I might learn something to explain why Rick was dead, and Casey Jordan, I decided to see what comforts and delicacies might be available at the Copa d'Oro, which was the name on the gold-and-white striped awning ahead of me. It protected the white wrought iron tables and chairs of the Hotel Miramar's restaurant bar. I was hungry.

The place exuded ostentatious elegance, to the extent that I wasn't sure they would let someone who had arrived on a beat-up motorbike sit in one of their chairs. Potted palms were strategically placed so that each table was intimately private but had an open vista of the beach and the sea. The patio surface was shining black marble tiles interspersed with white pebbles, and the tablecloths and the chair cushions were black-and-white-and-gold designer print fabric. I put my hands in the patch pockets of my beach trousers, tried for one of those petulant, bored expressions that fashion models favor in glossy magazines, and sauntered over to a table near the beach but still protected from the sun.

A waiter materialized from behind a palm and handed me a menu with a predictable gold cover, listings in four languages, and no prices. He had given me the ladies' menu even though I was alone. A little simmer of latent feminism made me consider insisting on a menu that had the prices, since I was obviously nobody's chattel, but I decided I really didn't want to know the prices. They would probably just spoil my lunch.

I ordered a margarita, since the afternnon seemed to present no more demands than maneuvering the scooter back to the ferry dock, or at most to the other end of the island and back, and settled down to decide between a fruit salad and a shrimp Louis. Something about the cavernous emptiness of the place made me not want to hazard the dressing, so the fruit salad won out. It was very good.

As I enjoyed my lunch, more patrons arrived, from the beach or the pool or whatever other Sybaritic pleasures might have been arranged for the hotel's guests to wile away a morning. I had simply been early. The dressing probably would have been fine. The margarita gave me a bit of a buzz, so I ordered lemon ice and coffee and enjoyed my view of the beach.

There were five or six cabañas close to the water; open, circular shelters with palm-thatched roofs. A few couples lay sunbathing. The only people moving were two boys running in the surf. They had appeared from around the point, coming toward the hotel, evidently seeing which one could run in the deepest water without falling or being outdistanced by the other. They were surrounded by great arcs of splashing spray.

One of the boys was dark and stocky, the other tall and fair with the gangliness that comes with rapid growth. The blond boy reminded me of Brandon, and I wondered again where he was. As the two came even with the hotel, they left the water and ran through the sand toward the restaurant. The blond boy had reminded me of Brandon because he was Brandon.

Since I was in the shade of the awning and two potted palms, and he was in the bright sunlight, Brandon didn't recognize me until he was even with my table and about five feet away. He stopped so suddenly that the other boy ran into him.

"Uh . . . I've got to go now, Javier, " Brandon said to his companion. "Tell your mother . . . tell her my aunt is here so I won't be having lunch with you. Thank you anyway."

The other boy looked at me curiously. "OK," he said. "See you later." He continued through the restaurant to a table where a woman was sitting with a young girl who looked so much like him that it had to be his sister. Brandon sat down in the chair across the table from me.

"Brandon Henshaw," I said, "you are something else. How in the world did you get here?"

"You are something else yourself, Mrs. Pritchard," Brandon said. His eyes still had the same wide stunned expression they had had when he first saw me, and I realized that while I had had some notion that he knew about Isla Mujeres, he had no reason at all to suspect that I did, or that it would occur to me to come there.

"I just came to remind you that you have nine hundred thirty-eight hours of detention time."

"Right. Three-oh-five in room one-oh-eight. What are you doing here?"

"Having lunch." The waiter arrived with my dessert and coffee. "Do you want to order something?"

Brandon ordered a cheeseburger and when the waiter left seemed to be groping for a place to begin, much as I was. "Look," he said, "I guess we've got some things to talk about, but could you do me a favor first? Just pretend to be my aunt for a minute and meet Javier's mother?"

"Can I know the scenario, or do I just improvise?"

"Well, my mother is quite ill, she thinks. We're staying in that hotel over there. Not the next one, the one farther over. Probably you came to take care of her. Something like that."

"That's what Javier thinks?"

"No. Javier's mother thinks that. Javier knows I'm down here by myself. I met him on the beach the day before yesterday. He's been helping me look for Felipe."

"Then you haven't found Felipe?"

"No," he said. "Here she comes." Brandon got to his feet. "Señora Gavito, I would like to present my Aunt Caroline," he said in Spanish. I decided that I did not speak Spanish.

"How do you do," I said. "I'm so pleased to meet you."

Javier was behind his mother, making faces at Brandon in an effort to find out who I really was, but Brandon ignored him.

"How is the mother?" Señora Gavito asked. "We are worried. . . ."

"She seems to be feeling a little better. I'm glad

74

Brandon has had some company. Very good of you."
We shook hands and smiled at each other. Señora Gavito's English, fortunately, was not good enough to sustain
a conversation, so after we had murmured how glad we
were to have made each other's acquaintance, she returned to her table and Brandon sat down again. His
cheeseburger arrived and was consumed.

"Can we go now?" Brandon asked.

I said that was fine with me, paid the bill with a
traveler's check that barely covered it, and we went
rattling off down the road on the old Vespa.

When we got back across the causeway, I saw a lane
cutting off to the left, a straight palm-lined road that led
across to the eastern shore of the island. I turned that
way, and in a few minutes we emerged onto a long
straight deserted beach. I stopped the scooter and we
found a shady place to sit, leaning against the trunk of a
downed palm.

"Who goes first?" Brandon asked.

I took two palmetto spines and broke one in half, then
concealed them behind my back while I arranged them
in my hand so only the tips protruded. "Short one first,"
I said, and held my hand out for him to choose.

He drew the longer frond, so I went first.

7

WHEN I'D FINISHED telling Brandon how I'd happened to be sitting in the Copa d'Oro having lunch, starting from the last time I'd seen him a week and two days before, he was silent for a few moments.

"Felipe isn't here," he said finally. We were sitting side by side looking out at the sea, but the weariness in his voice made me look at him.

"Well, you are here," I said. "You can't do more than your best."

"I thought he'd be here."

"Tell me how you got here."

"Well, when I got out of Juvenile, I went to the flats to see if Alfredo was out planting rice. He said they'd moved out of the camp. I hung around until he was done working and went home with him."

"Had they heard anything?" I asked.

"They'd heard something, but not much. Felipe had called an uncle in Morelia. He didn't say where he was calling from except that he was in Mexico. He asked his uncle to tell his mother that he was all right. She went to the telephone office in her village and called a neighbor in the camp to tell Señor Ramos. I sure thought that Felipe would be here."

"You must be worn out." I wanted to put my arm around his thin shoulders. I could have if he were a child, and I could have if he were a man, but he was some place in between that I couldn't get to, some place where his best friend was his only emotional connection to the world.

"So, anyway," he continued, "I showed Señor Ramos the locket and the piece of paper. He'd never heard of Isla Mujeres, and he didn't know anyone in the Yucatan. I said I was going to look for Felipe and I needed the money we were saving. I stayed there all night."

"You had money there? At the place by Sutter Buttes?"

He nodded. "Felipe and I are going to start a business, a video arcade. We'd saved nearly a hundred dollars. We kept it in a coffee can in Felipe's room. Alfredo knew it was there, so he took care of it when they left the camp."

"You can't have come all this way on less than a hundred dollars," I said.

"I still have most of it left," he said. "Seventy-three dollars. The next day I hitched a ride to Sacramento, only the man who picked me up was going to meet someone at the airport, so he wasn't going all the way into town. I told him I'd ride along and maybe get a ride with someone going from the airport into the city. I didn't want to be out on the highway any more than I could help it."

"Because of the highway patrol?"

"Right. Anyway, there was a flight leaving in a couple of hours for Mexico City, so I thought, Why not just try to get on it?"

"Brandon, that's crazy. You can't just walk onto an airplane."

"I did. It's a lot easier than trying to get on a bus without paying. There were four or five families with children. Nobody really looks at kids after they're old enough that they don't fall down all the time but not old enough to be traveling alone."

"That's what the sheriff said. He said it was hard to find lost kids because people didn't notice them."

"Also, one of the families had a pair of identical twins. Girls. You know how people stare at twins."

"I didn't know there were any flights between Sacramento and Mexico City. Harriet and I drove into San Francisco."

"I think this was some kind of charter. That might have been why they weren't checking very carefully. Most of the people seemed to know each other. Maybe it was a club or church group. When they announced that it was time to board the plane, I got between two of the families and hoped they'd each think I belonged with the other one."

"And you went through all of the security checks that way?"

"I wasn't carrying anything. That's another reason why it worked. Everyone was concentrating on checking the luggage. I didn't even have a bag. The only places where I could have been stopped was the door where a lady was checking boarding passes, and then when I got onto the plane and they were taking tickets and showing people to their seats. But the lady who checked the boarding passes was talking to the man putting the bags through the conveyer, and when I got on the plane there were three stewardesses taking tickets. They each thought I was part of one of the families that one of the others was seating. I really did just walk on."

"But you didn't have a seat," I said.

"That scared me at first. I was afraid all the seats would be full and they'd find out I'd just sneaked on. But the plane wasn't more than three-fourths full. There were a lot of empty seats. I went to the back of the plane and stood there looking at the magazines they had until everyone was on the plane and the signs came on that said to fasten the seat belts. I slid into an empty seat in the middle section and stayed there. They even gave me a coke and brought me lunch."

"But what about passport control?" I asked. "What about customs? Don't tell me you just walked through those."

"I ran, actually. Getting off the plane was a lot harder than getting on. I tried the same thing in the line where they checked the passports or visas, going ahead of a family, but I guess the man counted the number of kids they had listed. I heard him yell at me to stop. I took off and ran up an escalator by the baggage claim. I went into a bathroom and waited until I thought they would have stopped looking for me. Customs wasn't any problem because I didn't have a suitcase. I just waited for a family from another flight and walked through. I even stayed with them and got a ride into the city in one of those vans the hotels send for people on tours."

"Why didn't you stay in the airport and get a connecting flight for Mérida?" I asked. "It sounds to me like you had a pretty good system."

He grinned. "There's a difference between being lucky and being crazy. I was already in trouble in California, so it didn't make that much difference, but I wasn't sure what trouble in Mexico might be like. I had money. I figured I could get the rest of the way on a third-class bus. Actually I only went as far as Veracruz on the bus. I bought a ticket for only that far because I thought I might get a boat from there, but I got a ride with some people from Kansas instead. They had a camper and they were driving all the way to the Panama Canal. They didn't speak any Spanish and were trying to find some distilled water for the lady's contact lenses. I helped them talk to a pharmacist, and they said I could ride with them. It took three days, but I slept in the cab and they slept in the camper when we stopped. They brought me all the way to the ferry dock, even though it was out of their way."

"I bet you told them some great stories to explain how

you happened to be traveling through the Yucatan alone.''

"I told them the truth, but they didn't believe me. They thought I was running away, but the man said he'd been on his own since he was twelve years old and it was good to see a young person with 'gumption' was what he called it. They even invited me to go to Panama with them.''

"How are you sure that Felipe isn't here? It's not a big island, but there must be places . . . ''

"I don't think so. Javier and I have been over all of it.''

"You met Javier two days ago?"

"On the beach. The day after I got here. He was really bored, and his mother was glad to have someone for him to speak English with because he's supposed to take some big test when he goes back to school after the Easter holiday, and he hasn't studied very much. I told him about Felipe, and we've been over every place on the island at least twice. There's something I want you to see.''

"What is it?"

"I don't want to tell you. I want to see if you think the same thing I think.''

"Where is it?"

"Down toward the other end of the island and on the east side. We can ride down there on the bike.''

On the other side of the town the vegetation started getting thick. The road ran close to the sea, but even so there were places where the dense tropical growth closed in on both sides like a wall. Inland was impenetrable jungle. Occasionally there were side roads, hardly more than wagon tracks, leading off toward the interior.

"Turn around," Brandon yelled into my ear. "We missed the turn. That was the road back there.''

We bounced down the rutted track for about three

80

hundred yards before the going got so rough we abandoned the bike and went on foot. Brandon stopped when we could see the open sky ahead.

"You go on. I don't want to go down there again. There's a shack by a little cove. Go down and ask directions, or ask him if he's seen someone . . . just so you get a look at him," Brandon said.

"Who's 'him'?"

"The man in the shack. He came out with a shotgun the last time Javier and I were there and told us not to come back, so I don't want him to see that I'm with you."

"Thanks."

"You don't have to go down there."

"I'm going."

There was an old truck at the end of the road, and after that a path leading down to a small beach and a crescent-shaped cove. The shack was on the southern side of the little bay. A man sat on a bench by the door, mending a net. He watched me as I walked toward him, his face impassive. I asked him if this was the road to the Mayan observatory, and he said no. He volunteered nothing. I saw what Brandon had wanted me to see. Above the pocket of the faded and torn pair of coveralls that he wore was a darker area of fabric, a circle with two pointed ovals, as though a patch or emblem had been removed, leaving the darker cloth beneath. I apologized for intruding and went back along the path to the protection of the jungle.

"What do you think?" Brandon asked when I reached him.

"The same thing you think," I said. "I think that man is wearing coveralls that came from the McGraw Orchards. It's a coincidence, but it's not all that strange. The McGraws have a place in Cancun. They might have brought the uniform down here for one of their servants, who gave it away when it got worn out. Or maybe that man stole it. He looked capable of that, and worse.''

"Doesn't it seem to you like there's a lot of connections between the McGraw place and the east coast of Yucatan?'' Brandon asked.

"The only connection we know of for sure,'' I said, "is that Jensen and Harriet McGraw have residences in both places. Which is not illegal as far as I know. We both thought that the scrap of paper in Felipe's locket meant Isla Mujeres, but just because we both made the same assumption doesn't make it correct.''

"Right.''

"Look, Brandon, don't forget that Felipe got word to his mother that he was all right. He may even be with her by now. You say he's a smart kid, so if you could figure out how to get out of Juvenile Hall, what makes you think Felipe couldn't get away from whoever took him from Fair Oaks? If someone did. We really know almost nothing.''

"Right.''

"Will you go back with me, then?''

"I don't think either of us will be going anywhere today,'' he said.

"Why not?''

"Listen.''

I heard a steam whistle in the distance. "That's the ferry whistle isn't it?''

"Yes. The ferry comes twice a day. The first time you were on it. The second time you're not.''

"The last ferry is leaving?''

"Right.''

"I'll have to get to a telephone and call Harriet so she won't worry. It was stupid of me not to check the schedule, but I can't say I'm sorry. It's a beautiful island.''

"You could probably get a room at the hotel where my

82

mother is supposed to be, but I know a better place,"
Brandon said.

"Where?"

"Where I'm staying. It costs fifty cents a night for a
hammock, but we have to bring something back for
dinner. Showers are free with cold water, about a quarter
for hot water, and you have to have your own soap."

"I could hardly turn down a deal like that," I said.
"Let's get back to town and rent the scooter for another
day. And show me where the telephone office is so I can
call Cancun."

Harriet laughed when I told her I'd missed the ferry.
She said she thought the schedule was arranged by the
hotel owners. We planned to meet at the ferry dock at
noon the next day and drive down the coast to Tulum.

Since we had most of the next morning, Brandon and
I got some masks and snorkels and fins at the rental shop
while I was arranging to keep the scooter another day. I
was glad to see that he was starting to enjoy being a
tourist. We followed the smell of fresh bread down a side
street to a bakery, where we bought five torpedo-shaped
loaves fresh from the oven, and a dozen sweet little
panitas.

The *hamucca* park where Brandon was staying was
just north of town, right on the beach. There was a large
enclosure with a stake fence around it, and two long
open sheds for hammocks—fifty cents a night if you used
their hammock, twenty five if you had your own. A third
shelter had a fire pit and served as kitchen for the
residents. It was open on two sides, with three showers
backed against the side that had a long sink for cleaning
up after meals.

"Loaves and fishes for the multitudes," said a rangy
bearded American when he saw us coming with the
bread. He held up a large bonito in one hand and his
spear gun in the other. "Good luck today."

The young people at the *hamucca* park shared their resources and fixed a communal meal in the evening. A couple from Argentina were making a pot of soup from sand crabs and kelp. Not a hopeful prospect, I thought, but it did turn out to be edible. There were two Danish girls who had been given some vegetables when the market closed and were making a salad. A Japanese boy who said he had been traveling for two years brought in a bunch of small green finger-sized bananas, which he wrapped in their own leaves and put in the edge of the fire. After they had roasted they tasted like a cross between a yam and a popsicle stick.

By the time the meal was ready it was getting dark. We had all stopped to walk down to the water's edge and sit silently on the sand to watch the sun set behind the dark mass of the mainland. I know that the company and the evening had much to do with my memory of it, but still I believe that was one of the best meals I've ever had. We sat around the fire afterward and the Argentinian man played the guitar while his wife sang and the Japanese boy played a reed flute.

Somewhere close by I heard a dull thump, and then another, and everyone cheered. Brandon and the American man dashed off into the darkness and came back with two coconuts. A bottle of vodka appeared and the coconuts were split with a machete and heavily spiked. We passed them around until the vodka and coconut milk were gone, and then divided the sweet chewy meat.

The conversation consisted mostly of an exchange of information. Those headed north told how to get by in Guatemala, San Salvador, Nicaragua, what to see in Peru, how to make a little money in Bolivia. Those headed south reported on where to stay in Mexico, the cheapest way to get through the US to Canada. They were part of a brotherhood of wanderers, temporarily, or for some, as a way of life. They concentrated their energies not on making money but on not needing it.

"I'm living on forty cents a day," the American said, "and it wouldn't be that much if I weren't staying here in the park. But it's good to have company once in a while."

"But sooner or later you must run out of money, even at that," I said.

"When I do I work for a month. That usually does me for the rest of the year."

Someone said that there was always something that could be taken across the next border and sold for more in the next country. The Japanese boy said he never worked. He just watched the exchange rates and when he sensed a devaluation coming he traded for yen and then back into the local currency. Bill, the American, said that you could do that with dollars or Deutschmarks or yen, Swiss francs, too, but that it was too much like work for him to watch the financial reports every day.

Some of them had been there for over a month. "We came for a weekend two months ago," one of the Danish girls said. When they found a place like that, with plentiful food and beautiful beaches, they weren't in any hurry to move on.

The fire died down and people went to the sleeping sheds or had a last walk along the beach. Bill joined Brandon and me, and we walked north along the curve of white sand, the stars brilliant and close.

"If you weren't Brandon's girl," Bill said, "I'd invite you to have a drink with me at one of those fancy hotels."

"It would have cost a month's expense money," I said.

"Mrs. Pritchard is not my girl," Brandon said.

"Yes, I am," I said, "so you better call me Carrie."

"That's what I figured," Bill said, "but I thought I'd try."

"I like 'Caroline' better," Brandon said, and quit hanging back and then walking ahead as though he thought maybe he wasn't wanted. Bill had given us the chance to get something straight: one reason Brandon and I were together was that we liked each other. After that the awkwardness was gone.

In the morning Brandon and I woke in our hammocks before the sun had cleared the slight rise in the center of the island, and were on the scooter heading for the south end, where Bill had said the best diving was. It took us a while to get the hang of breathing through the snorkels and clearing them of water after diving without choking on salt water, but when we did we had the key to a silent world so amazing that we swam and dived until we were exhausted.

There was a coral reef not more than twenty-five yards out, and in and around it lived brilliant fish. Some seemed to live alone, others in pairs, and others in small or large schools. There were quite large flat blue-gray fish, looking like slightly oval dinner platters, that schooled together by the hundreds, like a great fog bank hanging in the water. They let us swim among them without any fear, slipping out of reach only when we tried to grab one. Then, for mysterious reasons of their own, they would suddenly turn like a single creature and dart off, only to hang motionless again several yards away.

Many of the fish were fluorescent, particularly the ones who lived deeper in crevices in the coral. There were long slender striped fish, purple and iridescent green with a dot of crimson by their gills, and angel fish with their feathery fins moving gently, holding them steady under the ledges. The reef came so close to the surface of the water that we could find places to stand and rest, our fins protecting our feet from the sharp coral.

That morning! If you have half a dozen such experiences in a lifetime, I think them sufficient recompense for whatever else may happen to you. And so we had that day.

I tried to get Brandon to come with me on the ferry, but he wanted to stay on Isla Mujeres a few days longer, just in case. He did promise that he'd call me in the morning, and that he'd come back to Fair Oaks with me. I couldn't blame him for wanting to stay on the island as long as possible. He would be with Javier, and with Bill and the others at the *hamucca* park. He waved me off on the wallowing ferry, and I stood looking back through the haze of exhaust fumes, watching him get on the scooter and head back south along the road to find Bill and learn how to use the spear gun.

There was an extra crossing on Sundays, so a crowd had already gathered at the mainland dock to take the 1:00 P.M. ferry. As the boat approached the land, I was looking for Harriet's car, so I didn't notice Felipe until he had already seen me and had started moving rapidly away through the crowd. I wasn't sure at first that it was Felipe. I watched him while the ropes were secured and the gangplank was laid across for the passengers. He had moved behind a group of men. He didn't realize that I had spotted him, so I was able to get within a few feet of him to be sure that it was him before he started running. I didn't have a chance of catching him.

"Stop!" I yelled. "Stop that boy! He took my wallet."

A group of German tourists were standing near the road. One of the young men dropped his rucksack and intercepted Felipe, grabbing him by the arm.

"I'm sorry," I said to Felipe when I got to them. "Please. *Por favor*. Don't run."

Felipe looked at me with an expression blank with fear. The young German looked bewildered. "I made a mistake," I said, and he walked off, shaking his head.

"I have to get on the ferry," Felipe said.

"Brandon is there," I said. "He's on the island. He's staying at the *hamucca* park."

For a moment Felipe's expression changed. "Brandon is here?" Then the fear was back. "He has to leave. They'll kill him. Please, I can't talk to you. They'll see us."

"Who will? Felipe, don't go." But he was gone.

"Who was that?" Harriet had come up behind me. "Is there some trouble? Should I send Mata after him?"

I hesitated. From what Brandon had said, Felipe was not a boy who could be frightened easily. But he was frightened. I saw Mata coming up behind Harriet, and something about his face decided me, something hard and closed. "No. No, of course not. I was just asking the boy . . . if he knew about the ferries tomorrow."

"Sunday is the only day they have an extra ferry. Come on, you'll love Tulum."

I did not love Tulum. I have only the vaguest recollection of a large area, walled on three sides and open to the sea, with a temple pyramid that seemed to face out, waiting. I knew the dread was my own, but it seemed to belong to the place, to have lain there along the ground for centuries since the lookout first sighted the Spanish ships that would bring their empire down.

"You seem distracted," Harriet said. We were down on the beach, having the picnic that Mata's wife had fixed. "Did you meet some young man on the island? I hope so. It's time, you know."

It took a moment for me to realize that Harriet suspected a romance—at first I thought she somehow knew about Brandon. "Yes," I said. "Yes, I did." I put together a rather garbled story, giving Bill the credit for having swept me into a love-at-first-sight dream, including some details about going diving. Since Harriet had provided me with the excuse for going back to Isla Mujeres, I decided to capitalize on it.

"We must have him come over for dinner then," Harriet said. "I've got some good news, too. Jensen is going to be able to get away after all. He called yesterday and should be here tonight."

There were, as Brandon had observed, rather a lot of unexplained connections. I watched Harriet's pleasant face as she looked out at the breakers rolling across the reef. Was it possible that this sturdy creative woman could have anything at all to do with the fear I'd seen on Felipe's face? I had a strong urge to tell her everything, to get her to help me get Brandon and Felipe and take them home immediately. But, again, I saw Mata approaching and I remembered that I didn't know a safe place because I didn't know where the danger was coming from.

8

JENSEN MCGRAW ARRIVED at about eight o'clock that evening. I had never been particularly fond of Jensen, nor had I disliked him; he had not been of interest. Now, however, he was of considerable interest. He was a taciturn man, of medium height, medium build, medium everything as far as physical appearance went. His thin hair, which had probably been sandy when he was young, was now a yellowed gray and, with his freckled skin and pale blue eyes, contributed to a general washed-out impression. I remember hearing one of the town gossips say that she didn't understand how such a wimp had made it from dirt farmer to millionaire—with the implication that she did know. But I was fairly sure that although Harriet's family had been wealthy, they had not been as wealthy as Jensen was now.

"Harriet tells me you've been to Isla Mujeres," Jensen said as he handed me a scotch. He had brought it to the balcony, where I was looking out over the sea.

"Yes. It's very beautiful. I'd never been diving before—it's like visiting another world."

"So I hear. Never tried it myself. Never got around to learning to swim when I was a boy."

"It's very good of you and Harriet to have me here. I could hardly have had an experience like this without your kind invitation." I left it at that, holding against the urge to babble that my nervousness and Jensen's silences invited.

"Glad you could come," Jensen said. "Didn't know

until the last minute that I'd be able to come down. Harriet was pleased that you could come with her."

Having exchanged the obligatory pleasantries, we let Harriet take responsibility for the conversation during dinner. Seeing them together, which I seldom had, I had a sense of how they functioned as a team. Harriet reported such information as Jensen wished to have made public, in her pleasant, no-nonsense way, and he left her to her art and her comforts.

"Jensen and I are going to see Riano tomorrow," Harriet said. "Do come along with us. His work is worth seeing."

"You're going to Mérida?" I asked.

"Oh, no. Riano lives quite near. Between here and Tulum. He hardly ever goes to Mérida—doesn't like cities. Señor Carillo comes down here when he needs to see him. I want to see what Riano thinks about that jade mask. Jensen brought it with him."

"Brought it with him?" I asked in astonishment.

"Yes, and the two terra-cotta pieces," Harriet said. "I didn't care that much for the stone figures, did you, Jensen?"

"No," he said, his attention remaining with the chicken molè that Mata's wife had served.

"How did you happen to meet this Riano?" I asked Harriet.

"I worked with him for a while," Harriet said. "I saw some of his work in Mérida. Not his reproductions, his own work, and asked about him. When I learned that he lived here on the coast, I asked him if he'd teach me his techniques. Had to have Mata ask him—he doesn't speak anything but Mayan. We didn't need to speak. He's one of the finest craftsmen I've ever met."

"And what do you do with his work? Is it all for your house?"

"Oh, heavens no. I can't resist keeping some, but

mostly they're sold. Since we've been coming down here, Jensen's started an import business. The orchards don't make much now, and Sam Jordan takes care of everything anyway. Most of the pieces go to the east coast. It's not high volume of course. Jensen has been considering an outlet in San Francisco, but frankly I don't want the competition.''

I did want to see the workshop, more because of my suspicions about Jensen's activities than for any genuine interest in Riano's work, but I also wanted to get back to Isla Mujeres. I let the subject drop without making a commitment. We retired early, and although I still felt uneasy, the long day in the sun had so tired me that I fell asleep immediately.

When I woke it was because of a tap on the door and Mata's wife softly calling my name. "Señora Pritchard, telephone.''

Jensen was already having breakfast in the L-shaped front room as I went in to take the call.

"Caroline? It's Brandon. Felipe's here. Can you come back to the island?''

"Yes. Good morning.''

"You can't talk, right?''

"Right.''

"Felipe came to the camp last night. He couldn't stay. We only talked for a few minutes. I don't know what's going on, but it's bad, whatever it is. I think we should get out of here, all of us.''

"I think that's a wonderful idea. Of course I'd like to.''

"He's going to come back tonight. He told me to stay around the hotel with Javier today. He's scared, but he couldn't tell me why. Only that I had to stay away from him and he'd get back tonight. Can you come?''

"It sounds like fun. I'll be on the afternoon ferry. See you then.'' I hung up the phone and tried for a happy smile. "I hope you don't mind," I said to Jensen, "but I've accepted an invitation to do some diving tonight on the island."

"Was that your young man?" asked Harriet, coming into the room from the kitchen.

"Yes. It was Bill. He's arranging for a boat out to the reef. I said I'd catch the afternoon ferry."

"Good for you. I was just asking the cook to fix us a lunch. If you want to come along and see Riano's workshop, we can all go and we'll drop you at the ferry in the afternoon. And see if this Bill would like to come for dinner tomorrow. We'd like to have him, wouldn't we, Jensen?"

"What can you see diving in the dark?" Jensen asked.

"I understand that many of the fish are phosphorescent," I said. "I've heard that it's very beautiful." I'd never heard any such thing, and thought it unlikely, but I was counting on Jensen's lack of interest in diving and Harriet's lack of interest in any type of disagreement.

"It's probably snipe hunting anyway," Harriet said.

"Snipe hunting? What in the world is snipe hunting?" I asked.

"When I was a girl, that's what it was called when a young man wanted to get his girl friend to go off to some private place."

Riano's workshop had a huge kiln, which Harriet said he had constructed himself, in the center of a barn-sized enclosure with roof and walls of thatch supported by poles. Wooden shelves around the walls held his molds and implements, and a long wooden trestle table was his work space.

The man was quite small, as most of the Mayans seemed to be. He acknowledged our arrival with a nod, but did not leave his work. Harriet was quite at home and went immediately to a shelf in the back where several pieces stood. They were circles of primitive dancing figures.

"Tarascan," Harriet said. "Or rather they're Riano's work inspired by some of the Tarascan dance-circle pieces. His are much better from the standpoint of design. This is where he keeps the pieces that are ready to be fired. With that big kiln he usually only fires once or twice a week. It takes the whole day. This next firing will probably be just smaller pieces. He has to control the temperature differently, depending on the volume."

Riano had two assistants, young men who were working in the back with a huge vat of slip, or liquid clay. "Hi, Harriet," one of them called.

"Hello, Edward. It's good to see you're still here. This is Carrie Pritchard, a friend from California. Carrie, Edward Blake. Edward's studying with Riano, like I did," Harriet said.

"Well, I won't be for much longer if this goes on," the young man said. "This is getting more like a factory than a studio. Riano has us spending all our time with these molds. I haven't time for my own work."

Harriet moved away and picked up an unfired piece to examine. Evidently Edward didn't know her well enough to realize that she had no time for complaints—she didn't make them and she didn't listen to them.

"I didn't come all the way down here to work on a production line," Edward said to me since mine was the only ear available.

"How did you happen to come down here?" I asked.

"I was studying at the Art Institute in Chicago when I saw some of Riano's work. They had an exhibit of meso-American art with the work of contemporary artists and sculptors included. I wanted to work with him. But by the time I got here he'd started doing reproductions for export. It's not like when Harriet was studying with him. I might as well be in one of those neighborhood craft

94

shops where they make bunnies and pixies for bored housewives to glaze.''

"Why don't you go somewhere else, then?''

"Ahhhh, it's not all that bad. The beaches are great.'' He went on stirring the slip, then began pouring it carefully into a mold.

Riano had left the figure he was working on, draping it with a wet towel to keep the surface moist, and was talking to Jensen, with Mata serving as translator. Mata had carried in a large box, and Jensen was lifting out the objects I had seen in Señor Carillo's shop.

My misgivings seemed foolish to me as I observed the activity in the workshop. Certainly if there were anything sinister going on, they wouldn't have included me so casually in the process, nor the grousing Edward. Probably some official was looking the other way in order that Riano could have access to original pre-Columbian pieces, and probably Jensen made it worth the official's while—Harriet had implied that in Carrillo's shop—but that was hardly sinister. Jensen McGraw again seemed what he had seemed before: a rather ordinary although quite successful businessman.

"Harriet? Could you come over here for a minute?'' Jensen called to his wife, and she joined their discussion. They were talking about the mask. I gathered that Riano was not in agreement with some suggestion that Jensen had made, because he was shaking his head. Harriet spoke with them for a moment and then shrugged and came over to me.

"Do you like Riano's work?'' she asked me.

"I wonder why he spends his time with reproductions when his own work is so good?'' I was looking at a terracotta figure of a woman carrying a basket on her shoulder. It echoed the old Mayan pieces, but it made quite a different impression. It had a feeling of dignity, but a

95

dignity born of endurance and suffering rather than power and wealth.

"Is this for sale, I wonder?" I knew I probably couldn't afford it, but I wanted it. Rick would have understood it. Maybe I understood it too. Anyway, I wanted it.

"There's a mistaken notion that artists are visionary romantics," Harriet said. "On the contrary, I've found that the good ones are firmly rooted realists, very practical about their finances and their time. Riano doesn't take on any work that will make more demands on his time and energy than he considers worthwhile. He just refused to do a reproduction of the jade mask because he doesn't think any other material would do it justice, and it would be too time consuming besides. I thought perhaps it would turn out that way, but it's such a magnificent piece that I thought it worth a try."

I bought the terra-cotta figure, even though I could ill afford the price, which, at that, was probably only a fraction of what it should have been were I not a friend of Harriet's. She told me that Jensen would arrange the shipping.

By the time Harriet and Jensen dropped me off at the ferry terminal, I had relaxed. Their interest in Mayan art and the import business connected with it seemed legitimate, and Mata seemed merely passive and silent, as was typical of these Indians.

Brandon was waiting when the ferry docked, anxious to get back to the *hamucca* park in case Felipe should come. We got bread and cheese so we wouldn't have to leave again once we got there.

"What did Felipe say?" I asked when we were sitting on the beach watching the sun drop low on the horizon behind dark bars of clouds.

"It was after midnight last night. The man who runs the park came and got me. He doesn't let anyone in who hasn't paid or isn't a guest of someone who's paid. Otherwise I guess you might as well sling your hammock out anywhere. Anyway, he said someone was asking for me by the gate, and it was Felipe. He'd seen you at the dock, he said."

"He was frightened. He ran when he saw me. Why would he be frightened of me?" I asked.

"I don't think he was frightened of you," Brandon said. "I think he's afraid of what will happen if he's seen talking to anyone at all. Particularly to an American. He was only here for about five minutes, and he kept looking around. All he said, really, was that I should stay around people, and not try to see him until he came to me."

"Did you tell him that you were going to call me?"

"No. I thought about that afterward. I thought about it most of the night, and what I thought, finally, was that when he comes here, if he comes, we should get out of here. Just stay together and get on the ferry in the morning and get back to Butte County, whatever that means—Sheriff Pratcher and Juvenile Hall, and probably deportation for Felipe and his family, I don't know. But he'd be safe."

"What makes you think that Felipe will agree? We don't know anything about what's going on. And whatever he knows has him very frightened," I said.

"We just have to wait," Brandon said. "Three is better than two."

So we waited. We built a fire on the beach, afraid of going into the *hamucca* park lest Felipe wouldn't be able to get in when he came. If he came. We talked. We told our lives' stories and talked about what we wanted the rest of our lives to be like. I told Brandon about what my life was going to be like in San Francisco, about the apartment I'd have overlooking the bay, with sheer white curtains that the breeze would blow gently on sunny mornings, about the sounds of fog horns at night in the rain. About the job I'd have as systems analyst in a large office high up in a glass-and-steel building. About the concerts I'd go to, the opera, the theater.

"I guess you'll be getting another boyfriend, then," Brandon said. "I'll have a hard time getting to San Francisco."

"Why? Couldn't Felipe handle the arcade by himself some of the time? You could trade off, couldn't you?"

"It's going to be a lot of work. It's not like a shop. There'll be a lot of traveling involved, particularly for Felipe."

"I don't understand. What traveling will there be to running a video arcade? How are you going to finance it, anyway?"

"Felipe's going to win some tournaments. Get a name as someone to beat. Of course he won't be competing in our place. We don't have to buy the equipment. The companies that make the machines lease them. We already talked to the man who put the machines in the 7-11 and the Round Table Pizza. We go around with him sometimes. The money isn't in the machines as much as in the tournaments."

"So Felipe will be like the golf pro at an exlcusive course, is that it?" I asked.

"Right. And I'll handle the business end. If you run an arcade right, you can have different kinds of competitions going all the time. There's a place in Old Town in Sacramento that this man took us to—"

"What about the gambling laws? Sounds like you'll be in trouble if you're charging entrance fees and giving prizes."

"Well, you have to be careful, but it's no different than a ping pong tournament, or chess, or something like that. You know, people who play the games want to be the best, get a trophy or a ribbon or something so they can show people. If there's betting on the side, well, that's not anything the management can be blamed for.''

"The management being you and Felipe.''

"Right. All we need is the money to lease the space. We've got it all planned.''

"I don't want to sound like a doomsayer,'' I said, "but who's going to lease space to a Mexican boy who's in the country illegally and a fourteen-year-old kid who ran away from Juvenile Hall?''

"Nearly fifteen. There are a few details to be worked out.''

It filled some of the time. I watched Brandon's face as he talked. Something about the firelight made it possible to see the face of the man he would become. The shadows emphasized his jawline, made it look firmer than a boy's, and the emerging cheekbones. He wouldn't be shirt-advertisement handsome, but he'd be a good-looking man. His voice had only a slight edge of his customary irony, just enough to acknowledge that the plans he and Felipe had made were going to be difficult to accomplish, but not enough to disparage them.

Bill came out to see what we were doing out on the beach, and went back to get a dog-eared deck of cards that he had in his rucksack. We played poker for beach pebbles until it became obvious that each of us had more pebbles than we'd all three started with. You can't play poker without credibility for your currency. Bill decided to turn in. Brandon and I took turns going up and down the beach for more driftwood to keep the fire going. After midnight we didn't talk much. It was nearly 2:00 A.M. when Felipe finally came.

We were sitting there, staring at the coals, when we heard his voice behind us. He told us to pretend we were going back into the camp, but to follow the fence down to the shadow of some palms. Brandon and I did what he said, shamming stretches and yawns as though we had tired of our little beach party, as we covered the coals with sand and walked toward the entrance to the *hamucca* park. Then we ducked down, close to the stake fence, and went as quietly as we could to the deeper darkness under the palms.

"Felipe," Brandon said, holding his arm as though he could keep him safe by the physical contact. "We've got to get out of here, all of us."

"No," Felipe said, "but you must go. I think so."

"What's going on?" I asked. "What are you doing?"

"I take things to Sonora," Felipe said. "On the bus. On the train to Mexico City, then the bus. That's what they want me for."

"What things?" Brandon asked.

"I don't know. There was an old suitcase and a box with a rope around it, like baggage a poor person would have. But inside were metal cases. I don't know what was in them."

"Who gave them to you?" I asked.

"It's the man in the shack by the cove, isn't it?" Brandon asked. "Who is he? He has a funny accent."

"I don't know. I know he's not Mexican. They call him Queso. I have to get back—he might wake up." Felipe looked around.

"No," Brandon said. "We'll stay together and get on the ferry in the morning."

"Felipe, what happened on the McGraw place? How did you get into this?" I asked.

"I saw the plane. It was early, and I was by the river, going to the rice flats. I thought it was going to crash, but it landed in the hay field. Two men got out and took out some boxes. Then someone hit me."

"Did you see the man who hit you? Do you know who it was?" I asked.

"I heard his voice, but I never saw him. When I woke up I was tied to a chair. I didn't even know where I was, but it was one of those old cabins. They had a blindfold over my eyes, and a bag over that. He wanted to kill me—"

"The man who hit you?" Brandon asked.

"Yes. The Mexican, he was the pilot, said they could use me, and the one who had been with him in the plane said he wouldn't have had to talk on his way to Sonora if he'd had someone with him. Anyone who heard him knew he wasn't Mexican."

"Could you tell where he was from?" I asked.

"No. He and the man who hit me all talked the way Queso does. The pilot was Mexican. They all talked in English. The man who wanted to kill me said it was too dangerous, that it was better to get rid of me."

"I guess you didn't agree with him," Brandon said. He still had his hand on Felipe's arm. Even in the night it was pale against Felipe's dark skin.

Felipe smiled for the first time. "I said I was sure looking for a job, and if they had one I would do whatever they told me. When they knew I could understand English, the argument started all over. I think the man who came with the pilot was the boss. He said I'd be even more useful if I could speak English. He said they couldn't kill people there because that was too dangerous."

"You mean they came from someplace where it was all right to kill people?" I asked him.

"I don't think the boss knew about the boy who was killed. He left the next morning, but we didn't go until night."

"The boy? You mean Casey?" I asked.

"I don't know his name. He lived near there, I'd seen him. The man who wanted to kill me said he wanted to be back in town before the plane took off. I was still in the cabin and the pilot had gone out to get the plane ready. The other man came back—I still had the blindfold on and the sack—he untied me and dragged me out with him. Then he yanked the blindfold off and I saw the boy. 'You see that,' he said. 'I did that with your knife, and I've got another knife for your father.' Then he took me back and the pilot was waiting.''

"But you didn't see him?" Brandon asked.

"He was behind me. He twisted my arm so I couldn't turn around. He shoved me into the shack and said, 'Give me twenty minutes.' The pilot and I went over to the plane—he didn't tie me up, but he made me put the blindfold back on when he landed the plane and I had to keep it on until we got to Hermosillo.''

"What happened after you got to Hermosillo?" I asked.

"He showed me the place, a store that sold radios and televisions, and said that was where I was to deliver whatever I was told to bring. Then we went back and he brought me down here, to Mérida, and we took the bus and the ferry here. Queso didn't like it. He said they should have killed me when they first caught me. They had the same argument all over again. The pilot said he couldn't wait if the shipment wasn't there. It came by boat that night and I left the next day with it.''

"Why did you come back? Why didn't you keep going?" I asked.

"He said he'd kill my father.''

"I told you last night," Brandon said, "they can't find your father. They're safe over at Sutter Buttes.''

"You found them," Felipe said.

"Only because I knew where Alfredo was working. They wouldn't know that.''

"We don't know what they know," Felipe said, and I had to agree with him. We didn't know what they knew because we didn't know who they were, except for the man called Queso. "I've got to get back," Felipe said. "You go tomorrow.''

"I'm not going without you," Brandon said.

"Felipe," I said, "I think Brandon's right. We should all be on the ferry in the morning. We can be back in California by tomorrow night. We can call your father's lawyer from Mérida and he can arrange for protection for your family."

"How are Felipe and I going to get back into the US?" Brandon asked.

"Let Pratcher worry about that," I said. "He wants both of you. Those are nice folks at Juvenile, remember?"

"Right," Brandon said. "It will work, Felipe."

He was silent for a while. "You know my father's lawyer?"

"He's a friend," I said. "A good friend. Your father trusts him. All we have to do is get to Mérida and the telephone office."

"The bus will be waiting when the ferry gets across," Felipe said. He was silent again. Then, "All right. We'll go on the morning ferry. But I've got to go back now. If Queso knows I've been gone he won't let any of us go. I know it. I'll be there tomorrow when the ferry goes."

"Don't go back there," Brandon said. "If we stay together he can't do anything."

"No," said Felipe, "we can't risk it. The ferry doesn't leave until noon. That's too long. It's safer this way. Queso sleeps soundly, and he was drinking tonight. I got out and back last night without him suspecting anything. I think he trusts me more since I delivered the stuff and came back."

"What if you can't get here?" Brandon asked.

"I'll get here. I'll get here just before the ferry leaves. You just be ready." Before we could say anything else, he was gone, running up the beach and disappearing into the shadows.

9

"BUT WHAT IF he comes and we're not there? What if he needs help?"

"Eat your breakfast."

"You're not eating yours."

"Never mind that," I said. "Look, we already decided what we are going to do. There's no sense in jumping around like fleas on a griddle. The best thing we can do is act like laid-back tourists. If anyone did see us with Felipe . . . well, we just have to assume no one did . . . but if they did, the best thing to do is act like nothing is happening. Also, nothing is happening. We're just sitting here having breakfast."

Brandon and I had gone to the breakfast buffet at the Copa d'Oro after flopping about in our hammocks for the rest of the night, trying without success to get some sleep. A long morning stretched ahead of us. We thought we'd say good-bye to Javier and his family, maybe have a swim, act as casual as we could. The hotels seemed insulated from any possible danger by their very expensiveness.

Javier came down to breakfast with his family and a Frisbee. We abandoned our table with its barely disturbed plates to join them. The boys went out on the beach and I conversed with Señora Gavita to the degree that her command of English allowed, which was enough to tell her that we were leaving that day, that Brandon's mother needed medical attention, that we appreciated their concern.

Then Brandon and I decided to walk the beach. We went around the point and down the long straight stretch on the eastern side of the island. We heard the faint whistle of the ferry in the distance. Only an hour and a half more and we'd be on it.

"We can start back to the *hamucca* park now," Brandon said.

"OK. Let's cut across on the lane with the palm trees," I said, "the one we came over with the motor-bike."

Down the beach, probably three hundred yards away, we could see a small group of people.

"Bill likes to dive down there," Brandon said. "That's where he got the big bonita the other day."

Small figures were running toward the group on the beach. It was apparent that something of interest had happened.

"Maybe someone caught a big fish," I said. "We've got plenty of time. Let's go see what it is." I didn't want to spend an hour and a half waiting around the *hamucca* park and the ferry dock. It seemed to me we should arrive as close to noon as possible.

"No," Brandon said. "Let's get back."

We turned down the long lane toward the west side, the high sun throwing the shadows of the palm leaves in gently moving patterns on the white sand. We were nearly to the park when we saw the Japanese boy coming toward us.

"Did you see Bill?" he asked.

"No, wasn't he over there?"

"They came to get him earlier," the boy said. "Some-one drowned they said. They wanted Bill to bring his tanks over to bring the body up. It was caught under water in the rocks."

The world was caught in a freeze-frame for a moment.

The Japanese face. The trunks of palms with patterns of sunlight. White sand. The sea in the distance.

"There's no reason . . . " I started to say, but Brandon wasn't there. He was running.

By the time I got back to the end of the lane, he was a hundred yards down the beach, running. There was no need to run.

The body was partially covered by a piece of canvas. A fairly large crowd had gathered. Perhaps fifty people were standing around in small groups discussing the situation, as people do, the early arrivals getting a sense of importance from telling the latecomers what they know. Brandon was kneeling beside the canvas, the dark hand of the drowned boy clasped in both hands. He was rocking back and forth slightly, his eyes closed. Bill was beside him.

"Brandon. Brandon, you can't do anything," Bill said. "Come on, now. Come away."

"Leave him, Bill," I said. "Leave him awhile."

Bill stood up and we moved away from the little clusters of people around the body. "Do you know the boy?" Bill asked me. "No one seems to know who he is. He's not from the island."

"Yes," I said. "It's Brandon's best friend. From home."

"Take this," Bill said. "It was in his pocket. There's no identification."

He slipped me a sodden wallet, and I put it in the outer pocket of my purse.

"Do you know what happened?" I asked Bill.

"Not really. I went diving early this morning and got back to the park around nine-thirty. I'd only been back for a few minutes when two men came running in to ask me if I had my tanks ready. Most of the scuba divers were out and they wanted me to dive for a body. Some-

106

one had seen it while they were snorkeling, but couldn't get it up because it had lodged in the rocks."

"So you brought him up. How long was he . . ."

"Impossible to tell," Bill said. "Maybe two hours, maybe ten hours."

"Not ten," I said. And then I saw the dark face watching. He was on the other side of the body, staring at Brandon. He still wore the coveralls with the dark patch above the pocket. "Bill," I said, "I've got to get Brandon on the ferry. Can you take care of Felipe's body?"

"That's the dead boy?"

I nodded without taking my eyes from the face ten yards away. "His name is Felipe Ramos. His mother lives in a village called Cuitzeo, near Morelia. Ramos. There's an uncle in Morelia."

"I can take care of it through the church," Bill said. "The priest will help."

"Here," I said. "There may be expenses." I took a couple of travelers' checks and signed them quickly. "I've got to get Brandon out of here."

"I'll go with you," Bill said. "I'll get the priest on my way back."

"Brandon, we have to go. Now." I leaned over him. "Turn your head to the right and look."

He looked, and got to his feet. "But I can't leave him—"

"We have to," I said. "Bill will take care of the body. He's dead, Brandon. There's nothing more to do. We've got to be on that ferry in twenty minutes."

I took his arm and he moved with me, in stiff, jerky movements. I looked behind me and saw the man moving through the crowd after us. I turned and pointed at him.

"Do you see that man, Bill? That one, in the mechanics' coveralls? He killed Felipe."

"What in the hell is going on?" Bill asked.

"There isn't time to tell you. We have to get on that boat. Just be careful."

We made it to the ferry with a few minutes to spare. Bill held back to be sure that we weren't followed onto the boat. Finally the gangplank was pulled on board, the ropes cast off, and the engines began their muffled straining. The expanse of water that we thought represented safety grew wider behind us.

I don't remember getting off the ferry, and I don't remember getting on the bus, although we must have. I remember feeling cold, and that Brandon was shivering in the seat beside me, although the temperature must have been near ninety.

The first thing that I remember clearly was getting off the bus in Mérida. I looked past the people who were waiting at the side of the bus to retrieve their baggage and saw Mata beyond them. He was leaning against the wall and watching us. My first impulse was to grab Brandon and run. My second was that if he let me see him, perhaps he wanted us to run. Perhaps he wasn't alone.

"Brandon," I said, "the man against the wall over there is the McGraw's driver. Do you see him?"

Brandon looked past me and nodded. "The Mayan. Are you sure?"

"Sure enough. He may not be alone," I said.

"Right. What are we going to do?"

"I don't know about you, but I'm going to scream," I said. And I did. A screaming woman can get a fair amount of attention anywhere, but in very passive cultures like that of the Mexican Indians, the effect is gratifying. I had yelled and jabbered for only about three or four minutes before the police were there. Brandon kept talking to me, telling me to calm down, telling me everything was all right. We were pretty good. At least partially because once I started screaming I realized that it was what I'd wanted to do for a couple of hours.

Brandon explained to the police that I was his aunt and given to occasional bouts of hysteria that were usually kept under control by medication. He told them that he was sure that I'd be all right once I got onto the plane for Mexico City, where my husband was waiting for us. I looked back once we were safely inside the police car, but there was no one by the wall. Brandon made a show of getting a pill from my purse, a lint covered Tic Tac, and I calmed down as they drove us to the airport. The plane was leaving for Mexico City in half an hour, but there would be a three hour layover before the flight to Tijuana.

"Well," I said when we were on the plane, "we don't know who may be on the plane with us, but we can be fairly certain if there is anyone he doesn't have a weapon."

"All we know," Brandon said, "is that someone will probably try to kill us. We don't know who, and we don't know why."

"Maybe we know more than we think we do, if we put it together right," I said. "We haven't had time to think about it. Most of what we know is what Felipe told us last night. Someone in Fair Oaks is bringing something into the US from Mexico in a small plane, which either drops whatever it is, or can land on the McGraw property if necessary."

"Right. And it is brought ashore on Isla Mujeres at that cove where Queso stays, and then taken to the plane in Sonora. Sometimes there are men who go along, men who speak Spanish but aren't Mexican."

"Would you like something to drink?" the stewardess asked. "We have Coca-Cola, 7-Up, beer, wine. Mixed drinks are available." I wanted a scotch but settled for a Coke. Brandon had one, too.

"OK," I said after a minute or two, "you're right. We know just enough to get killed for, but not enough to protect ourselves."

"We'd better try," Brandon said. "Let's start by making some notes about the people on this plane. That way we'll know which ones are on the Tijuana flight."

We were sitting near the back of the plane, so I started with the dozen or so people behind us while Brandon went toward the front to have a look at the first-class section. Family of four, look German. Two women, Mexican, probably mother and daughter. Young people, possibly honeymooners. Two men, late middle age, gray and blue business suits. Lone man, early thirties, blond, wearing Hawaiian shirt and jeans. I walked toward the front, making no effort to conceal the fact that I was making observations and taking notes. If anyone was watching us, he would at least know that we were watching him. It might help. It might not. Actually it was already helping since it gave us something to do.

"Of course," Brandon said as we were going over our list and making a special effort to get a good look at any men traveling alone, "we're easy to spot. If they have anyone in Mexico City, all they'd have to do is have them get on the plane to Tijuana there. Or catch us at the airport."

"All that means is that we have to be careful. We knew that already. All we have to do is find an open place and stay in it, back to back if necessary, until the plane to Tijuana is called."

"We can't stay in open places for the rest of our lives," Brandon said.

"We don't know how long that's going to be."

"Right."

Talking about it seemed to help. Putting words on the things we knew and the things we didn't know made us feel like we were in control. I told Brandon about my experience with Harriet at Señor Carillo's, and about Jensen McGraw's import business, and my feeling that Harriet couldn't be mixed up in anything like this.

At the airport in Mexico City there was still a three-hour wait. Brandon and I went upstairs to the restaurant and got a small table in the back corner by the windows, which looked out on the loading area. We both faced the stairs, watching.

"Agent Q6R," Brandon said, "we have reason to believe that these earth energy forms are dangerous. It appears that they do damage to others of their kind—a most serious pathology."

"We are fortunate," I said, "that headquarters has fitted us with total protection under our human-skin disguises."

"We sure are," Brandon said. "I thought they were being ridiculous, but it seems their precautions may come in handy."

"No one seems to be noticing us. I guess our disguises must be convincing," I said. "I don't know how research arrived at them, but they seem to work."

We were on the planet doing field research. We were the first team from our star system to be outfitted to mingle with the earth creatures. Research had been good, but not perfect. They had proceeded on the assumption that the most densely populated area was the most important, and had set us down in Mexico City. We, however, had reason to believe that the main power centers lay elsewhere.

We were undoubtedly certifiable. We had much too much nervous energy to stay put for the entire time. Our new identities, completely impervious to harm as they were, allowed us to move about cautiously since our only fear was that we would be revealed as aliens and thus fail in our mission.

"So, Agent G39," I said, "what are—"

"Why don't I have two letters?"

"I have seniority, remember. So, Agent G39, what are our plans for complete assimilation?"

"First we enter the neighboring energy collective, since this odd planet splits the available sustenance into such units, or so it seems."

"And then?"

"And then we continue our experiments. We find a safe base of operations from which to pursue our studies and formulate our recommendations."

"Not an easy task," I said.

"Right."

We were down in the main waiting area by then, sitting with our backs to a wall and a large plate glass window to one side. "Brandon," I said, "you're a weird kid."

"You're right, of course," he said, "we have to use the name designations and all other expressions these humans use. It's dangerous to retain any of our own reference orientations."

"Brandon . . ."

"Now then, Caroline," he said, "research was correct in assuming that these outer coverings are not an integral part of the organism. What they did not realize was that humans, for as yet unknown reasons, have more than one such covering and carry them about in boxes with handles when they move any distance over the surface of the planet."

"That man was on the plane."

"Which man?" Brandon asked.

"There. Across from us. In the Hawaiian shirt."

"Yes. Well, there are others waiting for connecting flights," he said. "Those two by the counter were on the plane, too."

"But he was watching us," I said.

"That was research's idea in making one of us what the humans call an attractive woman, or foxy lady,

112

because that variety of human can most easily obtain help in difficult situations. I don't think they realized that the variety also causes difficult situations."

"You don't know why he's watching us."

"He's been looking at your legs," Brandon said.

I was wearing a pair of tan walking shorts and a blue shirt, both considerably the worse for wear since it had been a day and a half since I'd first put them on.

"Let's move again and see if anyone moves with us," I said.

We went back to the restaurant until the Tijuana plane was called. There were half a dozen of the same people who had been on the flight from Mérida, including the man in the Hawaiian shirt, who showed no further interest in my legs or anything else but slept all the way.

I tried to think through our next moves, but my mind felt numb with exhaustion. Even more disturbing than the fuzziness of being very, very tired was the veering away from the reality of our situation. Someone would try to kill us for what we knew. Someone who might be on the plane with us now. And someone who almost certainly was waiting in Fair Oaks. And the two of us were not exactly in any mental, emotional, or physical condition to deal with anything more demanding than breathing in and breathing out. We had to find a safe place where we could have some time to recover.

"I don't suppose they would consider beaming us up?" I said to my fellow agent.

"It's quite a ways," he said. "I think we're on our own."

It was well after midnight when we got to Tijuana, even though we'd gained three hours crossing time zones as we moved west. We got a taxi from the airport to the town, which was still ablaze with light and ablare with mariachi bands for the benefit of such tourists who still hung around. We took the taxi all the way to the border-crossing station. Our lack of baggage made the crossing easy.

"Just came over for the evening with my nephew," I said. "He's visiting."

"ID?" the customs guard asked.

"Driver's license. Credit cards," I said, showing him the contents of the plastic folder in my wallet.

"Any purchases?"

"No."

He waved us through. "What now, Q6R?" Brandon asked.

"Aunt Caroline."

"What now, Caroline?"

"There's a tram line that runs from here to San Diego," I said. "We're going to wait right over there in that store entrance for a while to make sure there's no one following us. Then we're going to walk up and get on the train. We're going to get off the train between here and San Diego and wait for the next one."

"Right."

The people crossing the border at that hour were mostly a bit the worse for the hour and their alcohol content. We waited about twenty minutes and then walked up the street toward the end of the tracks. There was a train just pulling in, which meant a wait before it started north.

We got off at San Ysidro and waited for the next cars to come. It was a long wait, but we were alone on the lighted platform most of the time. Not until about ten minutes before the next train did a few people gather at the station, a young couple with a sleeping child, an old woman, three teenaged Mexican boys. We started to relax a little, which meant we had to fight hard to keep from falling asleep before the train reached San Diego.

"Look," I said to the first taxi driver in line, "we've had our luggage stolen in Tijuana. Can you take us to a nice medium-priced hotel, somewhere on the water if possible, and one that won't give us a bad time about not having luggage?''

He nodded and we got in. His choice was called the Albertson, new but not flossy, about two blocks from the beach but with an unobstructed view from the upper floors. By the time I'd told my story to the night clerk, I was convinced it was true. My nephew and I had been visiting in Mexico and had had our luggage stolen while we were in Tijuana on our way back. We'd probably stay a few days in San Diego while we tried to recover it.

The clerk was sympathetic, expressed his doubts about our chances of seeing our belongings again, and gave us a family suite on the eighth floor, facing the Pacific. There were two connecting rooms, a large bath, and a tiny kitchenette. I stretched out on the bed while I waited for Brandon to use the bathroom, and when I opened my eyes he was sitting in the chair in my room looking at me.

"Sorry," I said, "I guess I dozed off. Looks like it's morning already."

"Wrong," he said, "it's afternoon."

"You mean I've been sleeping all day?"

"We both did."

"What time is it?" I asked. "For that matter, what day is it?"

"It's about two-thirty, I think. Wednesday. I woke up a couple of hours ago and got us some clothes. There's a shopping mall down the street."

"I can't believe I slept . . . what? Ten hours?"

"Probably you were tired." Brandon was wearing new Levis and a white tee shirt. His hair was still damp from the shower.

"What did you buy me?" I asked.

"In the closet and in the drawer," he said.

The dress was bright pink-and-red-and-orange striped

cotton. The underwear looked like it came from Frederick's of Hollywood. "Weren't you embarrassed?" I asked. "How did you know the sizes?"

"I asked one of the clerks at K-Mart to pick out stuff that would fit her. She was small like you."

"She must like bright colors," I said.

"I picked the dress," he said. "You never wear bright colors."

"Right."

"You can wear your shorts and blouse, then."

"Blackmailing fellow agents is not acceptable," I said.

There was shampoo in the bathroom, and a new toothbrush still in its plastic case. I stood under the shower for a long time. Safe. We were safe. I had used my mother's maiden name when we registered. No one could possibly know where we were. The striped dress was so different from anything I'd ever had on that I even looked like someone different—and I had to admit that with my dark hair, the colors didn't look bad. Brandon confirmed this with a whistle when I emerged from the bathroom at last.

We healed. We watched television. We went to the zoo. We ate a lot. We talked about our observations of the strange human creatures and planned our lives on this strange planet. We considered moving to some place like Akron, Ohio, and working in a truck stop out on the highway. Brandon could wash dishes and I'd wait tables.

"How about Washington?" Brandon suggested. "We'd be closer to the seats of power."

"Too expensive."

"Well, Alabama, then. How about Alabama? Sharecropping maybe."

"Let's not make any snap decisions," I said. "This will take some planning."

On Friday night there was an open-air Bach concert, a performance of the St. Matthew's Passion. We walked

116

back to the hotel along the beach without speaking, and I thought how odd it was that a man so long dead should reach into our lives that way. Almost like a guide. A voice speaking a different kind of language.

"Look," Brandon said, "that's where we came from."

The Milky Way stretched across the sky. We were looking deep into our galaxy. "Can you tell which is our star?" I asked him.

"Sure. I'm the navigator, aren't I? We'd be in bad trouble if I couldn't. It's that one. See the three bright ones there, in a right triangle? Now look to the left of the one at the top. Left and down just a little. The medium-bright star with a very dim one right below it."

We were looking up, and out toward the sea, and we didn't hear the footsteps behind us. They were standing there when we turned, four of them, too close. We started to walk around them, and they shifted their position so they still stood between us and the street, which was perhaps thirty yards away on the other side of a thick oleander hedge. Except for the two of us and the four young Chicanos the beach was deserted. Two of them had knives.

Brandon told them that we didn't have much money on us, which was true, but that they could have it, which was also true. They took what we had, except for a five-dollar bill I had in my skirt pocket.

"Now get out of here," the tallest one said to Brandon. "We want the whore to stay." He was tossing his knife from one hand to the other, and took a step toward Brandon.

I was wondering how loud I could scream, and whether anyone would be able to hear me over the sound of the traffic on the road, and what the reaction of the boys would be, when Brandon moved. It was a single move-ment, the reach for the knife and the sidestep around the smallest of the boys, the one to the left of the boy who had had the knife. Brandon had the boy's arm twisted behind him and the point of the knife by his ear.

"I'm not going to kill him," Brandon said. "But if the three of you aren't gone right now, he'll only have one ear."

The other three didn't move. The knife point moved and the blood started and the boy screamed, "He's cutting me. He's cutting me." And the other three were running.

"Start toward the street," Brandon said to me, and I did. When I was halfway there he let the boy go and came after me. We found an opening in the hedge along the highway, waited for a space in the traffic flow, and crossed to a coffee shop. Neither of us spoke for a while. I thought about whether we should call the police, and knew that we weren't going to so there was no sense talking about it. We ordered coffee.

"I think I'll have a piece of cake," Brandon said. "It's my birthday."

"How badly did you hurt him?"

"Not much. There's a lot of blood under that soft skin around the ears."

"You said you were good with a knife," I said.

"Not real good," Brandon said. "I think when you're scared, sometimes it makes you better. Felipe . . . Felipe and I used to practice trying to take a knife from each other when we were tossing it back and forth like that. He could beat me. That guy wasn't expecting anything."

"Is it really your birthday?" I asked.

"If it's April 10th it is. I think it's April 10th."

"Happy Birthday."

When we got back to the hotel I had a long hot bath, and then tried to read a book I'd bought that afternoon, a best-seller so large and so boring that I thought certainly it would put me to sleep. The door between our rooms opened.

"You're not sleeping," Brandon said. He came over and sat on the side of the bed.

"Brandon . . ."

"We actually could go to Akron, Ohio," he said.

"I know," I said. "Do you know that it would change everything?"

"Going to Akron?"

"No."

"How would it change things?"

"I don't know that. I don't think there's any way to know."

He sat by me silently for a while, and then went back to his room. I was glad he hadn't asked me to decide, because the urge to reach out and put my arms around him, to comfort, to love, had been very strong.

10

AT ABOUT SIX I got dressed and went out alone for a walk along the beach. The tide was out, and a feeling of desolation—"the vast edges drear/ and naked shingles of the world"—combined oddly with the freshness of the morning. Somehow the whole center of my life had shifted. It was a different life than it had been even three weeks before—or I was a different person. I wished that Rick could have been there and walked along the beach with me. I walked for about three hours, a long way.

When I got back to the Albertson and up to our room, Brandon was standing by the window, looking out. He turned when I came in, and I knew he had been able to start grieving for Felipe. Four days. It had nothing to do with me. Their friendship had just belonged to the two of them.

"I have to go back," he said.

"I know."

"Look," he said, "I know why you want to . . . go to San Francisco."

"Why I want to run away?"

"I wanted to, too. I didn't understand it before. But I do now." Brandon turned back to the window. "You don't need to go back to Fair Oaks. There's no reason, really."

"Oh, shut up," I said. "We're both going back. Look, I've been walking a long way and I'm hungry. Do you want to have breakfast sent up or go out? We've got a few things to decide."

"Why don't I get some eggs and orange juice and we can make our own breakfast?" Brandon said. "We haven't even used the stove. Might as well get our money's worth."

"Tell them at the desk we'll be leaving in the morning," I said. "We can phone later and get reservations on an early flight."

After we'd had our eggs and toast and were sitting with orange juice and coffee, with the light curtains blowing a bit in the breeze coming off the ocean as the tide came in, we had a look at what we were up against.

"What are we going to do?" Brandon asked.

"That's not the right question," I said. "Before we decide what we're going to do, we have to know what we want. That's what Mack says. He says you may not get what you want, but you're pretty sure not to if you don't even know what it is."

"Right. What if we don't want the same thing?"

"We negotiate, I guess. What do you want?" I asked.

"I can't decide alone," he said after thinking about it for a while, "but I know what I want. I want to find out what's going on. I want to find out who they are and what they're doing. I want to stop them."

"Good. That's what I want, too," I said. "That doesn't mean we can get it. The only thing we have for bait is our lives."

"You want it that much?" he asked me.

"That's what we're talking about, isn't it? It would be easy to go to the sheriff and tell him what we know. He'd give us protection and be sure that whatever was going on didn't go on anymore," I said.

"Right. And they'd lie low for a while, and then start whatever it is some other way. We'd never know. I don't think they'd even do anything to us," Brandon said.

"That's about what I was thinking," I said.

"But you don't want it that way?" he asked again.

"No. But don't forget, they've had four days, too. Maybe they've already pulled out."

"We should have gone back right away," Brandon said.

"Don't start that. It doesn't lead anywhere. We couldn't have, and we didn't. I'm just saying that it's a possibility," I said.

"So, what are we going to do? It's time to ask that, isn't it?" Brandon said.

"Well, let's see what we know. Whatever is going on, it looks like Jensen McGraw is involved. Either he's the one behind it all, or he's working with other people. My guess is that he's smuggling Mayan art, but I don't have any way to prove it."

"What would it take to prove it?" Brandon asked.

"I guess we'd have to find things in Jensen's possession that weren't supposed to be. It doesn't sound like something he'd allow to happen," I said.

"Suppose he isn't? Just for the sake of argument," Brandon said.

"Then I wouldn't know where to begin," I said. "Except out at the McGraw place."

"What about Jordan?" Brandon asked. "What if the Jordans were the ones involved? After all, he's in charge of the orchards, isn't he? McGraw hardly goes out there anymore. What if it's someone using the McGraw land and the McGraws don't even know about it?"

"Then we're really in the dark," I said, "but I hope that's the way it is. I can't believe that Harriet could be involved."

"So what are we going to do?" Brandon asked again.

"The hardest thing," I said. "Nothing. We're just going to wait. You're going to your aunt's house in Sacramento and I'm going . . ."

"No."

"What do you mean, 'no'? Where do you think you're

going? If you don't want to go there, you can go back to Juvenile. Brandon, this is dangerous. You can't go back to your house."

"Let me hear what you're going to do," he said, "and then I'll figure out what I'm going to do."

"What I said. I'm going to wait. I'm going to go home as though nothing at all had happened. As though I was just getting back from a holiday in the Yucatan. And I'm going to work Monday morning like anyone else. And wait."

"And if they kill you?"

"Then I won't have to think about it. Meanwhile, I'm going to try very hard not to give them the opportunity," I said.

"The only two people that we're sure know we were both on Isla Mujeres are Queso and Mata," Brandon said. "And as far as we know they don't come to Fair Oaks."

"So?" I asked him.

"So if we don't have any contact with each other, anyone who knows we were together has to be involved," Brandon said. "We have to split up here. Today."

"How do we keep in touch? What are you going to do?" I asked.

"Let me think a minute," he said, and got up from the table and stood looking out of the window. "You're right," he said finally, "or Mack's right. Once you're sure what you want, the other is a lot easier. I'm going down to the shacks."

"Brandon, you can't!"

"Think about it a minute," he said. "I can't go near the Ramos place. They might be expecting that. I can't go home. And if they bring anything in or take anything out with a plane, I'll know about it. Maybe I'll get a look at them. And it's the last place they'd expect me to be."

"It's also about the most dangerous place," I said.

"We already talked about the safe way," Brandon said. "You're going to be in a lot more danger than I am, because you're going to be out in the open. They'll know you're back. Nobody's going to see me. I've had a lot of practice not being seen."

"No. I don't like it. There wouldn't be any way to communicate with each other," I said.

"What part of this whole thing do you like?" Brandon asked. "Look, if you want to change your mind about what you want, that's one thing. But if you really want to find out who they are and what they're doing, then this is as good a plan as any. I'll catch the bus this afternoon and get into Oroville in the early morning. I'll get a sleeping bag and some food, get onto the McGraw place, and break into one of the boarded-up shacks so that no one will be able to tell I'm in there. I even know which one—I've done it before."

"So how do we keep in communication?"

"We don't," he said. "If they're watching you, it would make it twice as dangerous for me. Look, I'll figure out ways to let you know I'm OK. I promise. You'll know. But you have to promise me something."

"What's that?" I asked.

"Promise me you won't get killed."

"That's got to be more than a promise," I said. "It's going to be a pact. For both of us."

"We have to kill a chicken and drink the blood," Brandon said.

"How about orange juice? I'm willing, but we're a little short of time."

"Is there some more orange juice?" he asked.

"A little. Enough." I washed out glasses and divided the remaining juice. We both stood by the window.

"Caroline Pritchard, I promise you that I won't get killed," Brandon said.

"Brandon Henshaw, I promise you that I won't get killed," I said. We drank the orange juice.

"I'm going now," Brandon said. "I'll have to find the bus station, and I don't know what time the bus leaves, so I'll just wait there."

"Wait a minute," I said. "How much money do you have? You don't have enough." I went to the closet where I kept the big straw purse with my traveler's checks. I didn't like to carry it with me when I went out, so I usually just took a few dollars in my billfold. As I took the purse from the hook, I noticed there was something in the side pocket.

"What's this?"

"What's what?" Brandon asked.

"Oh." I remembered. I remembered the beach and Bill handing me Felipe's wallet. Then I had looked up and seen Queso, and I had forgotten that the wallet was in my purse.

"What is it?" Brandon asked again.

"It's Felipe's wallet. Bill gave it to me and I forgot about it. "Wow," he said, taking out a wadded clump of money. "Look at that. Those are hundred-dollar bills. Wait a minute. They aren't all the same. What's this one?"

"It must be Mexican," I said.

"No. Look, it says they're *'lempiras.'* And here, 'Honduras.' What was Felipe doing with money from Honduras?" Brandon said.

"What was he doing with that much money of any kind?" I asked. "Queso can't have known he had it."

"It looks like more than two thousand dollars. And there's a couple more of the other kind." Brandon was separating the bills and spreading them out on the table. There were twenty-two one-hundred-dollar bills, and five large Honduran notes.

"Money is sure durable," I said. "It was soaked in

seawater, and then dried out all wadded up, but it didn't fall apart."

"They use good paper. Look," Brandon said, "I'm going to take a little longer than I thought getting back to Fair Oaks, so don't worry about me."

"What are you going to do?" I asked.

"I'm not sure exactly," he said, "but I'm going to stay over in L.A. and find someone from Honduras."

"And?"

"Not much. Just talk to them."

"In Spanish," I said. "To see if that's where Queso is from. Will you be able to tell?"

"I think so. I talked with him twice, and I listened to him while Javier talked to him. The first time we were down there he didn't suspect anything. He talked quite a bit about what kind of fish he caught around there."

Brandon got the canvas flight bag he'd bought at K-Mart and came over and gave me a quick hug. "Well, Mrs. Pritchard, see you in room three-oh-five."

"One-oh-eight."

"Right."

The earliest flight to Sacramento was at seven the next morning. I was home by ten on Easter morning. I panicked in the Sacramento airport, which I guess was as good a place as any for it to happen. I had gotten off the plane and was carrying my little K-Mart suitcase down the corridor to the main part of the terminal when it hit me. I was terrified of going back to Fair Oaks.

I went into the coffee shop, had a cup of coffee I didn't need, and thought about all the ways that someone could kill me. A bomb in the Mercedes. Someone waiting inside my apartment with the knife that slid between the ribs and into the heart slick and sure. A sharpshooter with a rifle in some window across the street. What had been wrong with me that I had told Brandon I wanted to wait them out? All I wanted was to go to the police, tell

126

them everything that had happened, and ask for their protection.

It was over in about fifteen minutes. In the middle of trying to figure out how someone could poison my peanut butter, I remembered the four Chicano boys on the beach. Trying to figure out how you were going to die was a waste of time and energy. About all I'd observed with any certainty about my ability to guess future events was that I never could. No matter how much I might think I'd examined all of the possibilities, what actually happened was inevitably a total surprise.

I paid for my coffee and got a taxi. It took me as long to get the forty miles from the airport to my apartment as it did to get from San Diego to Sacramento. And cost nearly as much. When the taxi pulled up in front of the apartment, I had a small relapse, enough that my hand was shaking as I paid the driver, but nothing serious. There was no one waiting in the apartment with a knife. When I went down to the garage and started the Mercedes it did not blow up. The streets of Fair Oaks looked much as they had before I left, except that the people I saw were in their Easter finery on the way home from church. I headed for the clinic.

The X ray was still in the Velasquez file, and I blessed the receptionist's inefficiency. I looked at the picture again, but aside from being able to tell that it was a side view of someone's skull, I could see nothing either wrong or right about it. I called Dr. Lampson.

He was just having Sunday dinner and invited me to come over and have dessert with them, so I got in the car, which again did not explode, and headed for Oroville. I finally got around to noticing that it was a magnificent Easter Sunday in early April. The rice fields were a brilliant light green, and almond orchards were billows of white under a pale blue sky. A pair of kites bucked and dipped in the gusty wind.

The Lampson's place was a big Victorian frame house on an acre lot, the kind that ambitious young couples imagine they are going to restore on weekends but which simply engulf them in blown fuses and dripping faucets. Bob and his wife seemed to have conceded defeat long ago and had settled in blowsy domesticity with their four children, an English sheepdog, cages of hamsters and white mice, and aquariums of tropical fish. An evenly distributed layer of abandoned toys, clothing, books, and papers covered every flat surface.

We had lime Jell-O and Oreo cookies around the big oak dining room table, and over the bickering of the children I gave them a travel agent's version of my trip to Yucatan. Finally Bob suggested we go into his study to talk.

"This is very good of you," I said. "I wanted you to look at this X ray and tell me what you see."

He turned his desk light on and held the X ray in front of it, moving the picture slowly and making little interpretive "hmmms" about whatever he was seeing. He seemed particularly interested in the area at the base of the skull, and that was where he pointed first.

"There seems to be a concussion here. You see this line? I can't be sure, though. This isn't a good angle. It might be just a shadow. I'd have to get another shot to be sure."

"If it is a concussion, is it serious?" I asked.

"Hard to tell," he said. "It might have knocked him out. I'd have to see another picture."

"You said 'him.' You're sure it's a man?"

"Almost sure, from the size of the skull. Do you mind if I ask where this came from?"

"I found it in the file of the last patient Rick saw. Remember, Rick was killed the night Raul Velasquez broke his leg."

"You think this may be the man who killed Rick?"

"I don't think anything, really, but I wondered what the X ray showed," I said.

"Well," Bob said, "one thing it shows is that this man has had extensive plastic surgery. Whatever he used to look like, he doesn't look like that now. Probably his own mother wouldn't know him."

"How can you tell that?" I asked.

"Look here. And here. That darker area on the surface isn't bone. The bone has been built up artificially to alter the contour of the cheekbones. And here it looks like the nose has been broken deliberately and reset. It doesn't look like restorative surgery."

"You mean that whoever this is has deliberately changed his appearance?"

"That's what it looks like to me," Bob said. "If Rick saw this, he would have thought the same thing. And he certainly would have taken another X ray to check on the possible concussion at the base of the skull."

"So maybe whoever it was wasn't even aware that this X ray still exists," I said.

"And probably Rick asked him about the plastic surgery," Bob said. "I know I would have if I'd looked at this. Maybe this will give the sheriff something to go on."

"I don't want to tell the sheriff about it yet, Bob," I said. "This is all just conjecture so far. There might be a perfectly simple explanation. Maybe this is someone in the Velasquez family. Maybe Raul's father or uncle was having headaches, or got hit on the head, so Rick just took an X ray while he was there. Or maybe it was just misfiled. Look, will you keep it for me? I want to check through some more files at the clinic, and talk to the Velasquez family. If nothing turns up to explain it, we'll take it to Pratcher."

"I don't mind keeping it," Bob said, "but I don't see what harm it would do to turn it over to the sheriff now.

If something else turns up to explain it, then you can tell him about it."

"Frankly, Bob, my encounters with Sheriff Pratcher have been rather difficult. I'd rather be sure that it's something important before I talk to him. Please don't say anything to him until I've checked some more. At least until I've had time to talk to Señor Velasquez."

"All right, Carrie. I'll keep the picture here in my desk. But I think the sheriff ought to see it as soon as possible. I know he's abrasive, but he's not the worst we've had by a long shot. In fact, I think he's a good man. He's not stupid, and he's not lazy, and he's reasonably honest. I know he's not as progressive in his thinking as you'd like him to be, but . . ."

"Thanks, Bob. I'll get back to you before the end of the week. I'll either have an explanation of what the X ray is, or we'll take it to Pratcher's office."

It took me about fifteen minutes to convince Señor and Señora Velasquez that I hadn't come to get the money they owed to the clinic for Raul's broken leg, Rita's tonsillectomy, the delivery of their eighth child, and other services, but I finally got them to stop their protests and promises and listen to what I was trying to ask them: had anyone in their family been X-rayed for a head injury? They thought about it, talked about it, and reported that Raul was the only one who had ever been X-rayed at all, and that was just his leg.

I went back to the clinic, locked myself in, and started through the files. It was slow going. The first time through I pulled the ones for July and August that had entries in Rick's writing indicating X rays had been taken. Of course there was a possibility that the skull X ray had been misfiled at another time, so I pulled all the U-V-W files, too, under the assumption that it would be difficult to be farther off than that. At eleven-thirty I locked up the clinic and went back home, tired and glad to be tired.

In the morning it was good to be back at the high school. There was routine confusion before the first class, with kids lined up at the admissions window to hand in their excuses for absences before the spring break, to explain why they had forgotten to bring the excuses they needed, apply for absence forms, or otherwise deal with sins of omission and commission that had happened so long before—two weeks—that they had all but faded completely from teenaged memory spans.

Then there were the excuses and carbons of the forms to be filed, absence slips coming in from the first period class to be recorded on the day's attendance sheet, students trailing in late from early morning dentists appointments or faulty alarm clocks. All the details and trivia of my job were welcomed gratefully.

Jim Herrero stopped by my office during his free period to ask me how the trip to Mexico had been. I ran through the travel agent patter I'd tried out on the Lampsons the day before, and it seemed to work well.

"What's been going on around Fair Oaks?" I asked Jim. "What have you heard about Brandon Henshaw? Did the sheriff find him?"

"Not that I've heard," Jim said, "and it's almost impossible not to hear about everything that happens, so I guess not. Why don't we call the sheriff's office and find out?"

"Good idea," I said, and reached for the phone. The sheriff wasn't in, but his secretary took the message that I was calling from the high school to inquire about his success in finding Brandon Henshaw. I blessed Jim silently for giving me the idea to call.

So the morning slid by in a welcome blur of paperwork. I dealt with another flurry of activity at the admissions window during lunch hour and then went down to the cafeteria to get a sandwich and a carton of milk to take back to my office. I'd been back in Fair Oaks for over twenty-four hours and nothing had happened. I thought about it for a minute or two, and then I called Harriet. I wasn't sure that she'd be back, but she answered the phone.

"Hello, Carrie." Her voice was as friendly as ever. "I'm glad you got back all right. We brought your things when we came back on Friday."

I wondered if she was used to having houseguests disappear without a word of explanation, and if so what had happened to some of the others. "Is Jensen there?" I asked her.

"No. He went into San Francisco. He'll be back tomorrow if you want to talk to him."

"Could I come by this afternoon, Harriet? I need to talk to you."

"Of course. You know you're always welcome."

When I got there at four-thirty, Rosa answered the door and I followed her to Harriet's studio. Harriet was working on the figure of a little girl. She had barely begun, so only the rough contours of the figure were revealed in the clay. I watched her work while she told me how she planned to complete the work, who her client was, where she had gotten the idea for this piece.

"Harriet, I want to talk to you," I said. "It's something serious."

"Nothing unpleasant, I hope," she said. "Go ahead. I'm listening." She stepped back from her work and narrowed her eyes, circling the figure slowly. "I'm listening," she repeated.

"When I was on Isla Mujeres," I said, "I wasn't with a friend. I was looking for a Mexican boy from Fair Oaks who had disappeared. I had reason to believe he might be there, and he was. He was killed down there. That's why I left so suddenly. I was afraid the people who killed him would kill me."

Harriet gave no sign that she had heard. She moved closer to her sculpture and turned the rotating pedestal slowly. After a few moments I realized that she was not going to respond.

"I think Jensen is involved with whoever killed that boy," I said.

Harriet glanced at me sharply, but still didn't say anything.

"I talked to the boy before he was killed," I said, "and he told me that he had been kidnapped while he was down by the river on the McGraw Orchards property, and that he was taken to Isla Mujeres to act as a courier. Something is being brought into this country illegally in a light plane that can land on a concealed airstrip down there."

"That's ridiculous," Harriet said.

"Harriet," I said, "I have always admired you for your refusal to listen to gossip or complaints. But something ugly and violent is going on, and Jensen is involved somehow. You can't just ignore this."

"Carrie, dear, that's what people always say—'This is different, my problem is more important, my worries are more awful.' There's no need for it. I don't know what has happened, but you're letting your imagination run away with you."

"Casey Jordan was killed down there, Harriet. You must know that. He was killed the same way my husband was killed. A boy from here was taken to Isla Mujeres and killed, drowned, by a man wearing coveralls from the McGraw Orchards."

"Drowned? An unfortunate accident, it seems."

"I want to talk to Jensen," I said.

"Leave him a message if you wish," she said. "I'll have Rosa get your things."

Harriet gestured at her cluttered work table as she left the room, so I found a piece of drawing paper and wrote several sentences for Jensen, outlining what I knew. I folded it, and secured it with a piece of masking tape. When Rosa carried my suitcase into the room, I gave her the message for Jensen, and she showed me out.

11

WHEN I GOT to the Round Table Pizza at ten-thirty they were getting ready to close the kitchen. A surly girl at the counter looked at me as though daring me to order a pizza, and treated me to a relieved smile when I ordered a schooner of draft beer and took it to a booth in the back. The place was empty except for three kids playing the video games, an older couple finishing their pizza at a table in the center, and a Mexican boy in the booth in the back corner. I left an empty booth between us and sat facing the door.

When I'd gotten home from Harriet's, there had been a note from Brandon in my mailbox telling me to meet him at the Round Table. I wondered if he'd realized that Jensen must be involved, and, even if he had, why he would chance going out where he might be seen. I looked around to be sure there was no one but the Mexican boy behind me. He was wearing the required black leather jacket and those annoying sunglasses that look like mirrors. When I turned to look at him he started to get up and I turned away.

I knew he was standing by my booth looking at me. "Master of disguises," he said.

"Brandon! Good grief!"

"Good, huh? No so good in the light, though." He slid into the booth opposite me. "The hair dye worked OK, but that stuff that girls use to make it look like they've got a suntan made me look like I've got terminal jaundice. I had to get some theatrical makeup, too. It's all right at night.''

"When did you get back?" I asked.

"This afternoon. I left L.A. last night."

"Did you find anyone from Honduras?"

"Several people. Queso is from Honduras, or somewhere down there, I'm sure of it. And those bills are worth about fifty dollars each.''

"What do you make of it?" I asked him.

He shrugged. "Felipe said there were three of them with the same accent. Queso and two who stayed here when the Mexican pilot took him down to Yucatan. It's like trying to put together one of those puzzles with very small pieces—only the pieces don't match.''

"Did you get into the cabin on the McGraw place?"

He nodded. "There's no one around down there at all. You know, we don't know that they know that Felipe talked to us. We could be waiting forever and nothing would happen to us.''

"I thought of that," I said. "In fact, if they had known, I don't think we would have made it farther than Mérida.''

"So they probably know you're back, but they don't know where I am," Brandon said. "And if they don't know that Felipe told us anything, they'll continue the operation, whatever it is. So sooner or later the plane will come.''

"I went over to the McGraw's house and left a note for Jensen," I said. "I told him I knew a plane was landing at the orchards and that something was being brought into this country from Yucatan. And that I thought he must know something about it.''

"I knew we should have gotten the chicken blood," Brandon said.

"Oh, nonsense. It may just put us where we thought

we were anyway. There's no way to get at them unless they know that Felipe did talk to us.''

"What are you going to do next?" Brandon asked me.

"Wait until I hear from Jensen. He's supposed to be back tomorrow. What about you? What's the reason for the amateur theatricals?"

"There must be someone out at the orchards who is part of this," Brandon said. "There has to be. Either Sam Jordan or someone working for him out there. If the plane is coming in at night, then someone has to be there. They can't have that close communications, so there must be someone there who can hear the plane and go out with a light if it needs to land."

"Sounds logical, but what are you doing?" I asked.

"Hanging around. I'm going to ask for a job tomorrow, talk to as many of the men as I can."

"You think it might be someone from Central America?"

"There's a chance anyway," he said.

"Is your Spanish really that good? Won't they know that you're not Mexican?" I asked him.

"Pero no, señora. Hablo gringo," Brandon said, with his voice resonating through his nasal passages in imitation of the familiar speech impediment cased by a cleft palate.

"Well," I said, "I guess it's the pot and the kettle. Is it too late for the chicken blood?"

"Closing time," the girl at the counter said.

The last I saw of Brandon that night he was cutting across the empty parking lot of the shopping mall and then he disappeared around the corner by the Safeway.

I was wound up when I got home. Hardly more than a day and I could see that waiting was not something I was good at. Whether Jensen knew anything or not, he'd have to take some kind of action—either to get rid of me or to find out what was going on down at the orchards.

In case it turned out to be the former, I sat down and wrote it all down, everything Felipe had said before he was killed, the X ray that Bob Lampson had, Brandon's certainty that the men were from somewhere in Central America, Queso wearing the McGraw Orchards coveralls. I put it in an envelope and wrote on it that it was to be opened in case anything happened to me.

The next morning I dropped the envelope off at Mack's before I went to school. He wasn't entirely awake, but he growled and took it. I felt considerably better after that.

Harriet called just before I headed for the detention room at three o'clock. She said Jensen had gotten back and wanted to talk to me. I said I'd be there shortly after four, and spent the hour alternating between deciding to call Sheriff Pratcher and deciding not to call Sheriff Pratcher. Finally the fact that Mack had my letter and Brandon had my promise decided me.

When I got to the McGraw house there was a McGraw Orchards truck parked in front. Harriet opened the door and let me in.

"Hello, Carrie," she said, with no trace of the preceding day's coolness in her voice. "Sam Jordan came unexpectedly on some business about the orchards. And then the principal from the high school wants Jensen to call about a school board meeting. I swear I about need an appointment to see him some days. I thought we could have some tea while you're waiting. Rosa's fixing it."

I could hear the men's voices coming from Jensen's study. It was obvious that they were disagreeing about something. Neither of them was the type given to shouting, so to hear their voices, angry and loud, was unnerving. Rosa brought the tea tray, the cups rattling a bit. Even Harriet looked distressed, although she smiled and thanked Rosa and calmly poured us some tea.

"Have you plans for the summer?" she asked me, and I looked at her blankly.

"Summer," I said.

"Yes," she said, "you seem to enjoy traveling. I thought perhaps you'd planned a trip."

"No," I said. "I haven't made any plans."

I looked at the Chac Mool that was holding the tea tray. It seemed like the others I'd seen. How would one tell whether it was an original or a good reproduction? What would an expert look for? Probably there was some sort of technical device to determine the age. But stone was stone, surely. It was as old as it was. I was aware suddenly that Harriet had said something and I hadn't heard her.

"I'm sorry," I said, "I was woolgathering."

"I said that I thought you'd enjoy Italy," she said. "Florence is one of my favorite cities."

I couldn't hear the men's voices anymore. I took the cup from Harriet and set it down on the table next to my chair.

"Did you get the papers for Tim Jordan from Jensen yet?" Harriet asked. "Perhaps that's what Jensen wants to see you about. Sugar?"

"No, thank you. No, I haven't gotten the papers. But I don't think that is what Jensen wants to see me about," I said. I heard an engine start and wondered if it were the truck. Perhaps Sam Jordan had left already. "Do you think Jensen is ready to see me now?"

"Oh, he'll be out shortly I'm sure," Harriet said. "They're probably going over the books. Sam Jordan is a wonderful man, but Jensen says that accounting procedures are not his strong suit. Is the tea all right? I have herb tea if you'd prefer."

"It's fine," I said. I was not about to drink any of it. Looking at Harriet's determinedly cheerful face, I wondered for the first time whether she was entirely sane.

And then wondered what 'entirely sane' might mean. I had the same feeling about the room, with its lush tropical plants, rich carpets and cushions, and deep soft sofas, that I had about the Yucatan jungle. It seemed hard to breathe. I got up and walked around the room. I looked out of the window and saw that the truck was gone.

"The truck is gone," I said.

"I can still hear voices," Harriet said. "Jensen is with someone."

I could hear them, too, when I went back to that end of the room. Voices speaking in normal tones so that they were barely detectable in the living room. Then in a while I didn't hear them.

"Well then," Harriet said, "I'll see how long Jensen is going to be." She left the room and I heard her steps going back to the kitchen, heard her tell Rosa she could come for the tea things. Heard her steps crossing through the dining room.

Then her voice, "Oh my God! Jensen! Jensen, Jensen."

When I got to the door between the dining room and Jensen's study, she was kneeling on the floor beside him, holding him, the blood on her hands and arms and as thick on the front of her smock as it was on Jensen's shirt.

"Call an ambulance," she said. "For God's sake, quick."

I went to the phone and dialed the emergency number, but I knew it was too late. I told the operator to send an ambulance and the police, and went back to the study. I didn't have much time.

Beside Jensen's desk were three heavily padded containers. They were all open, and the Styrofoam packing was scattered on the floor. I reached into the first one and took out a familiar burlap-wrapped bundle. The second was empty except for a small amount of packing material. From the third I took another wrapped bundle. Below it, well protected by padding, was the ceramic figure I had bought from Riano. For a moment it was this odd incongruity, this curious little act of consideration, that stopped me. Harriet had told me that Jensen would arrange to have my purchase shipped.

"Why don't they come?" Harriet said. "Where's the ambulance?"

I took the three objects into the dining room, unwrapping the first bundle. I placed the terra-cotta figure of the Mayan woman holding a child on the buffet table. In the distance I could hear sirens. I went out into the yard through the open French doors in the dining room, walked through the side gate to the front of the house, and got into my car. I had reached the corner before I saw the police car in my rearview mirror. It came down Walnut Street and stopped in front of the McGraw house. I turned the corner.

Where would the jade mask be safe? Not at my place. I wasn't even sure why I had taken the mask and removed the Mayan figurine from the study. But whoever had killed Jensen has wanted them to be found there, and that seemed a good enough reason to see that they were not. Where would the mask be safe? In the next block I saw the food locker. Why not? I still had a compartment there, although I hadn't used it for months. It was so cold inside that my nostrils stuck together when I breathed, and I wondered if the cold would harm jade, but I didn't have time to worry about it. I fumbled in my purse to find the combination of the padlock, finally got the lock off, and shoved the bundle into the wire cage that still held a venison haunch one of Rick's patients had given him.

Back at the McGraw house I parked down the block and went back in through the rose garden and the French doors to the dining room. The sheriff was standing in Jensen's study.

"Where have you been?" he asked me.

"I felt ill," I said. "I didn't think I could go through all of this again. I started to go home, but I couldn't. Where's Harriet?"

"Upstairs," Pratcher said. "Dr. Lampson is with her. She seems to be in shock. What do you know about this?"

I told him everything from the time I had arrived at the house at about four-thirty up until the time I made the call to the emergency operator.

"You heard voices coming from the study after you looked out the window and saw that the truck was gone?"

"Yes," I said, "I'm sure of it."

"Could Sam have come back without your hearing him?"

"I suppose so. He evidently left through the side doors. Maybe he came back. But I know I noticed that the truck was gone, and then heard someone talking in the study."

"Miz Pritchard," Pracher said, "there have been three murders in Butte County during the past year that were committed the same way, and you have found all three of the bodies. Now that makes me wonder if maybe you know more about this than you have told me. I want you to come with me when we leave here."

"Carrie," Bob Lampson said from behind me, "you have to show the sheriff the picture."

"What picture?" the sheriff asked.

"An X ray," I said. "I found it in the file Rick had out the night he was killed. I thought there might be some connection, so I showed it to Dr. Lampson and asked him to keep it for me."

"There are laws about withholding evidence," Pratcher said.

"I didn't know that it was evidence, and I still don't," I said.

Pratcher gave one of his sighs. "Miz Pritchard, I could do just fine without any amateur detectives. If you have anything at all, just let me see it, please. Bob, will you get that X ray and bring it to my office before you do your autopsy?"

I wanted to find Brandon. He must have been out at the orchards when the plane came with the mask and the figures. Where was he now? Presumably I wouldn't have a chance to find out for a while. Pratcher escorted me out the front door and down the walk to his car.

"You wait out here," Pratcher told me when we got to his office. He indicated a chair in his secretary's office.

"No," I said. "If I'm under arrest, tell me what I'm charged with. Otherwise I'm going home."

The look of surprise on the sheriff's face indicated that he wasn't used to having people question his authority. He thought about it for a minute.

"I can keep you in custody," he said, "make no mistake about that."

"But it will take you a while to arrange it legally, won't it?" I asked him. "I want to call my lawyer now." I was counting on his lack of enthusiasm for any dealings with Mack.

The sigh. "You keep quiet unless I ask you to say something," he said, and held the door to his office open for me. There were two deputies and Sam Jordan waiting in the office.

"All right, Sam," the sheriff said, "what the hell is going on?"

"I don't know what's going on, Sheriff," Jordan said, "but I'd like to. Your deputy says Jensen McGraw is dead. Is that right?"

"I'm afraid it is, Sam, and you were the last person known to have seen him alive, according to his wife. I'm going to have to keep you here, Sam. Now tell me what happened."

"I didn't kill McGraw. I was mad as hell, but I didn't kill him."

"What were you mad about?" Pratcher asked him.

"There's something going on out at the orchards. Something that got Casey killed. Every now and again I've heard a plane flying low down there—never thought much of it. Thought maybe it was one of them pilots buzzing his girlfriend's house across the highway. But the night Casey was killed I heard it again, only like a plane was taking off. I remembered it later, remembered Tim had asked me what I thought it was down there. Couple days later Tim and I went there. Don't have much call to, usually. Nothing there but hay fields, and Sanchez takes care of them."

"Sanchez?" the sheriff asked. "I thought you didn't hire Mexicans except for picking."

"Don't if I can help it," Jordan said. "Sanchez has been working there for about three years. McGraw hired him. Speaks English, takes care of the alfalfa fields, keeps out of the way, mends fences. Until today I never had any trouble with him."

"What happened today?" Pratcher asked.

"I told you Tim and I went down there a week or so ago and had a look around. There's something odd down there by the river. Some concrete strips set close together into the hay field. You can't see them, just that the alfalfa looks ragged at the end of the field, but that's not unusual."

"Concrete strips? What do you mean, concrete strips?"

"Well, it's the damndest thing. Couldn't figure it out at first. They're about as wide as those curbs along the

144

side of a street in town, and set in every yard or so. Then I thought about hearing the plane. That's flat land down there, but it gets muddy after the rains. Those strips would give just enough support so that a plane could land across them if it had to," Jordan said.

"Get to the point, will you?" Pratcher said.

"So I just waited," Jordan said. "This afternoon I heard the plane, so I jumped in the truck and drove down there. I saw Sanchez out in the hay field waving at it."

"Did it land there?" the sheriff asked.

"No. But it came in real low. Real low. I never seen even crop dusters fly in that low. It dropped three boxes. Two on the first pass and then it circled around and dropped the third. Sanchez picked them up. He said it was something McGraw had asked him to do. I said fine, if that was the deal I'd take them to McGraw and ask him what was going on. And that's what I did."

"You took whatever it was the plane had dropped to Jensen McGraw's house this afternoon?"

"That's right. I asked him what was going on, and he said he'd arranged to have some shipments delivered that way. I said that was a pretty funny way to have anything delivered, and why didn't he use UPS like everybody else," Jordan said.

"Did he tell you what was in the boxes?" Pratcher asked.

"No. But you ought to be able to find that out yourself, Sheriff. I left them right there in Jensen's study."

"You still haven't told me what the argument was about," the sheriff said.

'I told McGraw that if I was managing the orchards, then I wanted to know everything that went on down there. And if he wanted to make private arrangements with Sanchez, or anybody else, then he'd better get himself a new manager. If whatever he was getting was on the up and up, there was no call to be dropping it out of airplanes, I said. He told me it was his land and he could use it any way he damned pleased. I told him to get another boy, and I left."

"What time was that?"

"I don't know," Jordan said. He'd said what he had to say and Pratcher didn't get any more from him except occasional monosyllables of agreement or disagreement.

"All right, Miz Pritchard," the sheriff said to me, "what were you doing at the McGraw house?"

"Harriet McGraw is a friend of mine," I said. "We'd been to their place in Cancun for the holidays. I stopped by to see her and we were having tea. I also wanted to talk to Jensen about a work-study program for Tim Jordan. I'd given him the forms before the spring break, and I wanted to pick them up."

"How long were you at the house before Jensen was murdered?"

"I don't know. It seemed like a long time. Maybe forty-five minutes."

"Did you see Sam Jordan at all?"

"No. I saw the truck out front when I got there, and Harriet said that Jensen was with Mr. Jordan. I could hear voices—they were talking quite loud, shouting, really. Then a little later on I heard voices talking normally. That was after I noticed that the truck was gone. Finally Harriet said she'd see whether Jensen was going to be much longer. That's when she went in and found him."

"You weren't actually with her when she found the body?"

"No. I stayed in the living room," I said. "I heard her call out, and I went to the door of his study. Then I called the emergency operator."

"And then you left the house," Pratcher said.

"Yes," I said.

"Now what about these boxes that were supposedly

dropped from some airplane," Pratcher said. "Did you see them when you went in after Harriet and saw that Jensen was dead?"

"I'm not sure," I said.

"What do you mean, you're not sure?"

"I remember seeing the boxes because I noticed the packing material had come out onto the floor. But I don't know when I saw them, when I was with Harriet or when I came back and you were there." Somehow a little uncertainty seemed like it would make a lie more plausible.

Bob Lampson came in and handed the sheriff the envelope with the X ray. "Do you need me here?" he asked.

"Half a minute, Bob," Pratcher said. "Tell me again about this and when Miz Pritchard brought it over to your place."

"She brought it over on Sunday afternoon," the doctor said. "She wanted me to tell her what I could tell by looking at it. I said it showed a possible concussion, but I couldn't be sure because of the angle. And that whoever it was had had plastic surgery, probably to alter his appearance."

"Damn it, Bob," Pratcher said, "why didn't you bring it over to me?"

"Caroline wanted to be sure that it was something important before she bothered you. She wanted to check some more to be sure it wasn't just put in the wrong file by mistake," Bob said.

"I don't see why I bother coming to work at all," Pratcher said. "If everyone else is going to make all the decisions, I might as well stay home and watch the soap operas on TV."

I personally thought that was a good idea, but joined in the thick silence that followed.

"OK, Bob, thanks for bringing it over," Pratcher said.

"I won't keep you. Now then," he said to me as the doctor left, "tell me about it."

"There's nothing to tell, really. The night Rick was killed, the last patient he saw was Raul Velasquez. That was the night Raul broke his leg. That was why Rick was at the clinic that late. So when I saw that X ray of someone's skull in the Velasquez file, it seemed odd. That's all. I thought maybe it had something to do with Rick's murder."

"So instead of bringing it here, you took it to Bob Lampson."

"I'm sorry, Sheriff. If I'd realized you were able to read X rays I'd have brought it to you," I said. I knew it wasn't a good idea to antagonize him, but I couldn't get past the way the man's arrogance irritated me.

"As a matter of fact, Miz Pritchard," the sheriff said, "I can't read X rays. I can, however, get ahold of someone who can, just as you did. I am a law enforcement officer, just as Bob Lampson is a doctor. Has it occurred to you that my services might be useful when people are being killed in Butte County?"

"Even though your department is unable to keep one fourteen-year-old boy in custody?" I felt like my mouth had been taken over by some infernal force. I certainly hadn't intended to say that. Pratcher got up from his swivel chair, walked over to the window, and stood looking out. Then the thought that was behind my baiting of the sheriff surfaced: Whoever had committed the murders knew that the game was over. When he had killed Jensen, he had ended whatever had been going on. There was no chance of getting at him now. And by tampering with the evidence, I had more or less made sure that Pratcher wouldn't be able to do anything either.

Pratcher walked back to his desk and sat down. For a minute I saw the face behind the Broderick Crawford mask he wore, and I knew that the feeling of helplessness

I felt was not an unfamiliar emotion for him. His sarcasm and mine came from the same place.

"I'll have one of my deputies take you home, if that's what you want," he said.

"Please," I said.

"I didn't kill McGraw," Sam Jordan said.

12

WHEN I GOT home, there was no message from Brandon. I drove out to the orchards and walked down to the shacks, but he wasn't there. When I got back to the apartment he was sitting on the front steps waiting for me.

"Come on in," I said.

He followed me up the stairs and flopped down in the basket chair in the living room. "Felipe would be alive if we hadn't gone down to Isla Mujeres," he said.

"Jensen McGraw would be alive if we'd gone to the sheriff as soon as we got back and told him everything we knew," I said. "Jensen was the only one who could have told anyone anything."

"Right." He sat there on the upper part of his spine, feet stretched out in front of him, hands jammed into his jacket pockets. "We messed up."

"Looks that way," I agreed.

"They weren't any more worried about us than about a fly buzzing. Whoever *they* are," he said.

"What about Sanchez?" I asked him.

"He's gone," Brandon said. "How do you know about Sanchez?"

"I was at McGraw's when Jensen was killed," I said. "I've been at the sheriff's office since then. Sam Jordan said a man named Sanchez had waved the plane in this afternoon. He said Jensen hired Sanchez about three years ago."

Brandon nodded and hoisted himself up to about the

center of his spine. "I talked to Sanchez this morning. Not for long. He ran me off. But long enough to tell that he's got the same accent. I was down in the shack when the plane came. Sanchez was out in the field and then Sam Jordan came barreling down there in his pickup. Sanchez said that the packages the plane dropped were for McGraw, and Jordan said that was fine, that he'd take them to McGraw and find out what the hell was going on. You were there?" He sat up a little farther.

I told him what had happened.

"What did you do that for?" he asked me when I told him about putting the jade mask in the freezer.

"I don't know," I said. "It seems stupid now. I remember thinking that whoever killed Jensen wanted those things to be found, so if they wanted it that way, I didn't want it that way. Primitive reasoning."

"And the other thing, the little statue, is still in the house?"

"Yes," I said. "There's so many other things no one would notice except Harriet. Maybe Rosa would, and maybe not. There were three other terra-cotta pieces on the sideboard where I put it. You said Sanchez is gone? What do you mean, gone?"

"Gone. When Jordan put the boxes in the back of the pickup, I decided to go into town. I thought maybe I could get into the McGraw house somehow and find out what was in them. I tried to thumb a ride but no one stopped and I had to walk the whole way. By the time I got there, there was a crowd out front. They were carrying McGraw's body out to the ambulance. I stood around for a while, still thinking maybe I could get into the house, but the police and the sheriff's men were all over. Then I realized that Sanchez was the only person who knew what was going on. By the time I got back out there he was gone. He left fast, so whoever killed Mc-Graw must have called him. The house he lived in out there looked like a hurricane had hit it, drawers pulled out, clothes thrown around like he'd packed in about five minutes.''

"That's it, then," I said.

Brandon slid back down to his former low. "Right."

"It's a little late, but I'm going to tell the sheriff everything," I said. "I wanted to talk to you first so you'd know."

"What do you think they were bringing in?" Brandon asked. "Drugs?"

"I don't know," I said. "I don't suppose we'll ever know."

"Maybe it really was just those statues and things," Brandon said.

"Maybe. But that doesn't make sense, really. What was Queso waiting for at the cove? And why would the killer have left those two pieces there? The jade mask alone must be worth thousands. And what was in the third box? Anyway, do you want to come with me when I talk to Pratcher?" I asked him.

"I guess I'll be back in Juvenile for a while," he said. "Look, I want to take the money Felipe had over to his family before we go to see the sheriff."

"Better keep the *lempiras* to show him," I said. "I'll drive you over."

We didn't talk on the way down to Sutter Buttes. I waited in the car while Brandon went in.

"Señor Ramos went down to Cuitzeo," Brandon told me when he was back in the car. "Alfredo is still here. He said maybe his father would stay down there, particularly with the money. That's a lot of money down there."

"So now what?" I asked him. "Do you want to stay at my place? It's too late to talk to the sheriff tonight. Doesn't look like there's any hurry as far as I can see. We can drive over to Oroville in the morning."

152

"Thanks, but I guess I'll go on home. See if my dad's OK," he said.

The house was dark when we got there. The grass in front had been cut and the trash cleared out of the yard. I thought probably the neighbors had finally managed to get some kind of court order to force Virgil Henshaw to clean up the area in front of the house.

"I don't think it was wrong to try," I said. "Just because you know what you want doesn't mean you'll get it. I'll call you in the morning."

"Right," he said, and got out of the car. I watched him until he got to the porch and had reached above the door to get the key and then let himself into the house.

The sheriff hadn't come in yet when I called at seven-thirty the next morning, so I went over to the high school and got through the morning rush at the admissions window before I called Brandon.

"Have you seen the newspaper this morning?" he asked me.

"No, why?"

"Better have a look at page six," he said. "If that thing you have in the food locker looks like that picture, it may change things."

"What are you talking about?" I asked him.

"Just look at the Sacramento paper, OK? Call me back."

The secretary in the administration office was reading Ann Landers when I went in to look for the copy the school had delivered.

"Mind if I look at the front section for a minute?" I asked her.

"I think Don has it . . . no, here it is," she said, handing it to me and going back to her reading.

"Pre-Columbian Masterpiece Missing," was the headline on a news service story datelined Mexico City. I took the paper back to my office. There were two pictures. One was of a jade mask in the Anthropological Museum. The other was a blurry photograph of an Indian boy holding what looked to be the mask I had first seen in Señor Carillo's shop and which was now in the Fair Oaks food locker. The article said that the missing art treasure had been turned over to authorities by an Indian farmer who found it over a month ago, but that it had since disappeared. Not until a few days ago had one of the museum's curators seen the photographs and realized that it was one of a pair of ceremonial masks, the other of which was in the museum's collection. The missing artifact was priceless, but might bring several million from the avid collectors who made the pirating of art treasures a profitable business.

I took the paper back to the front office. "I'm going out for a home call," I said to the secretary. She nodded without looking up from the comics.

When I got to the McGraw house, Rosa let me in and asked me to wait. She said that Dr. Lampson had just left and that she'd ask if Harriet wanted to see me. When she went upstairs I went into the dining room. The terracotta figure was where I'd left it. I took my sweater off and wrapped it around the statue.

To my surprise, Harriet did want to see me. She was sitting propped up against her pillows, an untouched breakfast tray in front of her.

"Carrie?" she said, and I realized she was nearly anesthetized with sedation. She spoke deliberately, like someone very drunk who was pretending not to be, and had difficulty forming the syllables of my name.

"Yes," I said. "There's something I have to tell you. Can you understand me?"

She nodded. "Can unnerstand. Don' feel anything. I can't . . . talk ver' well."

"Do you recognize this?" I asked her, placing the

figure of the Mayan woman holding a child on the tray in front of her.

She touched it lightly with her fingers, but didn't try to pick it up. "Señor Carill . . . Carillo," she said.

"This was in the boxes that were in Jensen's study when he was killed," I said. "This and the jade mask. I tried to talk to you before. Jensen was smuggling Mayan art into the United States."

"Jensen . . . din't unnerstand."

"Did you know?" I asked her.

"Din't unnerstand. Sometimes . . . I almost knew."

"You mean when you saw things and realized they weren't reproductions?"

"Jensen din't unnerstand . . . we din't need . . ."

I took the figure. "I'm sorry, Harriet. I really am sorry."

"Jensen was a good man . . . he worked so hard. He wan'ed to show my parents. Even after they died he wan'ed . . ."

"Harriet, do you have any idea who killed Jensen? Who was he working with? Was it Sam Jordan?"

"Jensen din't unnerstand, Carrie," she said again, slipping back against the pillows. I took the tray from the bed and set it on her night table. "Did you have to?" she mumbled, her eyes closing although she tried to keep them open.

I went downstairs and found Rosa in the kitchen. "Could you tell me who came here to talk to Mr. McGraw?" I asked her.

"I tell the sheriff," she said.

"I know, Rosa," I said. "Please. Whoever killed Jensen McGraw killed my husband, too."

She thought about that for a moment and then nodded, acknowledging the ancient right of bereavement. "Mr. Jordan come every week. Mondays he come, unless Mr. McGraw was away. Then when they have meetings about the schools the men come here. Sometimes the man from the school comes."

"From the high school? The principal?"

"Yes," Rosa said. "The head man. My girl goes to the high school. Carmen, she goes."

"The man called Sanchez from the orchards? Did he come here?" I asked her.

"There was another man, yes. Looked like Mexican, but he never speaks to me. He bring things for Mr. McGraw. Maybe Mr. Jordan send him."

I thanked her and told her I thought Harriet was asleep now. I took the terra-cotta figure with me. I thought about stopping at the food locker, but didn't. The mask was safe there whenever I wanted it, or whenever the sheriff did.

When I pulled into the staff parking lot I saw a solitary figure in a black jacket and mirror sunglasses sitting at one of the picnic tables under the oak trees between the school and the playing field. I walked across the lawn to him.

"You didn't call back," he said.

"Sorry. I wanted to see if I could get the terra-cotta figure. And I wanted to try to talk to Harriet again," I said.

"Did you?" he asked.

"Both. Let's go to Oroville."

"Wait. The jade mask that was in the paper, is that the one you have?" he asked.

"Looks to be," I said.

"That changes things, doesn't it? Whoever left it in McGraw's study for the police to find thought it was worth maybe a few thousand, right? They're going to want it back if they know it's worth millions."

"Brandon, remember what we talked about last night? All we've done so far is make things worse. Remember

156

what Confucius said, 'When you're in a hole, stop digging.' "

"Right. Did Confucius really say that?"

"I don't know. Somebody said it. I just said it. Let's go."

I turned back toward the Mercedes and saw that Don Marquez was standing by the window in his office, watching us. *"Sometimes the man from the school comes," Rosa had said. "The head man."* Well, of course, I thought impatiently, Don is the principal and Jensen was the chairman of the school board. Of course they talked with each other.

Brandon had followed my gaze. "He's been here three years," he said. "Like Sanchez."

"Brandon, that is completely ridiculous," I said. "Now get in the car. We're going to talk to the sheriff. You can tell him that you think the principal of Fair Oaks High School is committing all the murders in Butte County."

"It wouldn't take long to find out," Brandon said. "What if we were right this time? What could we possibly lose by finding out for sure?"

What had Jim Herrero said? "Supposedly the school board hired him because he's Spanish speaking, but he can't be bothered to go out and talk to the Mexican parents at the labor camp. He doesn't even talk to the Chicano kids." And his face—that oddly anonymous look. . . .

"What do we have to lose?" Brandon asked again. "A few minutes?"

"Brandon, it is not possible," I said. "Educators have their whole lives on record. Transcripts of where they went to school. All the places they've taught or been administrators. It just isn't possible. Now forget it."

"Caroline, if there's even a chance and we don't take it . . ."

157

"Oh, damn it, Brandon," I snapped at him, "I'm really sick of your stupid games."

I walked to the car, took out the little bundle wrapped in my sweater, and carried it into the school without looking back. I went straight to the administration office.

"I want to talk to Don," I said to the secretary's inquiring look.

"I'll see if he has time to see you," she said.

"I'll just be a minute," I said without breaking stride, and went into his office. I closed the door behind me. If I was going to make a fool of myself there was no need to stand on ceremony. Don was sitting behind his desk, looking through some papers.

"Carrie," he said, smiling his bland welcoming smile. "I'm glad you came in. I've got some ideas I want to talk to you about. I know you're not planning on being here next year, but you know more about our attendance problems than anyone else, and I've been thinking about making some changes in our policy so that . . . what's this?"

I had taken the terra-cotta figure out of my sweater and placed it on his desk. "A souvenir of Yucatan," I said. "I thought you might be interested in seeing it."

"Ah yes," he said, "I heard that you went down there with the McGraws. Jensen was a fine man. The community has lost one of its most valuable citizens. He was one of the staunchest supporters of our educational program." He picked up the figure and then put it down again. "I've always regretted that I never had the opportunity to study the fine arts. I can see that this is charming, however."

What on earth was I doing there? I was behaving like a mad person. "I'll be glad to . . . listen to whatever ideas you have about attendance policy," I said.

"I'm having my secretary type up the proposal that I want to present to the board," he said, getting up from his swivel chair and walking to the door to show me out. "I'll ask her to give you a copy. I'd appreciate it very much if you'd look it over and tell me what you think."

Just as he opened the door there was a crash of breaking glass, and voices shouting in Spanish in the front hall. Don went through the door and out of the office. I heard him ordering someone to get out of the building, and then the sound of running feet. I could hear him speaking in Spanish, asking someone who the other boys had been. I couldn't tell anything from his voice.

When he came back into his office he betrayed a momentary surprise at seeing me still there.

"Was there something else?" he asked.

I closed the door again. "The man who killed my husband . . ." I began. "There's an X ray. I think . . . that you killed Rick. The X ray will prove it."

"Carrie," Don said gently. "My dear." He came around the desk. My knees felt too weak to hold me up and I sank into the chair beside his desk. I would be committed, no doubt about it. He put his hand on my shoulder and patted it.

"Carrie," he said, "you've been through so much. The shock of finding Jensen . . . I'm afraid you're not thinking very clearly right now. Let me call the school nurse. . . ."

"Call whomever you like," I said, "but I am going to call the sheriff and have him come here immediately. He has the X ray and will bring it with him." I reached for the phone, ready to carry my mad scene through to its final humiliation of including the sheriff in the growing number of people who would witness my total mental collapse.

Don caught my wrist firmly. "I'm afraid I don't have time for that this afternoon. I have other plans." He moved around behind the desk and took a small pistol from the drawer.

Oddly enough, I felt not fear but an enormous sense of relief. Through nothing but blind stupid luck and equally blind obstinancy we had at least part of what we'd wanted.

"I don't understand you, Carrie," Don was saying. "Why are you doing this? Another hour—half an hour—and I'd be gone. Now I'll have to take you with me." He picked up the phone and told his secretary that he was not to be disturbed for any reason except to be told when his car arrived.

"That's hardly your style, is it?" I asked, indicating the gun.

"No," he said. "I dislike guns. They make noise and there's something . . . impersonal about them."

"Impersonal. I don't understand. What was personal about killing Rick? What harm had he done you?"

"Maybe that's not the right word. No, I think it is. Not personal in the sense of the relationship with the other person, but with the action itself."

"The artistry of it?" I asked. "The single clean thrust?"

"You do surprise me," he said. "Yes, that's it exactly. I was sorry about your husband, by the way. About the Jordan boy, too. They were just in the wrong place at the wrong time. Bad luck."

I stared at him, fascinated. He had stepped out of the oleaginous persona of the small town high school principal as easily as someone might shrug off a coat.

"What did you look like before?" I asked him.

"So there was another X ray. I thought I remembered his taking two, but I couldn't be sure. I kept blacking out." Marquez picked up a gold-framed picture from his desk. "I tell people that's my brother with my mother. The people who knew us think I died in the revolution."

"Too bad," I said, looking at the face in the photograph. "You were a handsome man. Now there's just something . . . indistinct about you. A nonentity."

He gave a dry laugh. "A very wealthy nonentity, however, which is a compensation."

"Where did you learn to use a knife that way?"

"One of your Marine officers taught me that. Special services. He'd had his jungle training in Vietnam."

"I don't understand," I said.

"No, I suppose not," he said. "That's fortunate. The ignorance of North Americans makes many things possible for us."

"You killed Rick because of the X rays?" I asked.

"That, and because he might have recognized my . . . client. His pictures had been in the papers a day or two before."

"There was someone with you?"

"Yes. An utter fool. We had a rough landing, and I'd had a good crack on the head. I passed out in the car driving into town and that fool panicked and took me into the clinic when he saw the lights on."

"Who was it?"

"No one important. One of Duvalier's boys who decided it was time to invest his share in California real estate."

The phone buzzed and he picked it up impatiently. "Please," he said, "I asked not to be disturbed. Oh. I see. Very well. Yes, have them wait just a moment." He hung up the phone and said, "It seems that the vice-principal has apprehended Brandon Henshaw, who was responsible for the vandalism which occurred a few minutes ago. I'm going to bring Brandon in here, and if there's any difficulty, any at all, I will kill him. Is that clear?"

He put the small handgun in his suit jacket pocket and went to the door. "Would you send Brandon in, please? Thank you, Hugh. I'll take care of it."

161

Brandon came into the office and Marquez locked the door behind him, taking the gun from his jacket pocket.

"I see you've captured him," Brandon said to me.

"I consider it unfortunate," the principal said to him, "that you haven't used that clever mind in more constructive ways."

"Like you have?" Brandon asked him. "I hope you don't consider me impertinent for asking, sir, but how did you get to be a principal?"

Marquez gave his dry laugh again. "It's hardly a challenge to run a small high school after you've run a country, but I wasn't legally qualified. Jensen McGraw was the chairman of the school board. He simply took a highly qualified applicant's materials and put my name on them. He told the board that he'd checked my references personally, and no one questioned him. As far as Jensen knew, my only aim was to establish a respectable citizenship in your country. You people are naive that way, imagining that all the rest of the world wants to emulate you."

"You don't mind having the Yankee dollar, I guess," Brandon said.

"Speaking of which," Marquez said to me, "I believe that you have another little souvenir of Yucatan. Is that correct?"

"No," I said.

"I have a permit for this gun. Things are working out quite well, you know," Marquez said. "Have you considered how justified I would be in shooting Brandon if he happened to come at me with a knife? I even have a knife for the purpose. It seems that the carved jade is considerably more valuable than I had thought. We might as well have it. Brandon and I will wait here while you bring it from wherever it is. Do not be gone long, as my car will be here soon."

"Don't do it," Brandon said. "Leave it where it is."

162

"You will come with me in either case," Marquez said to me. "The only issue under discussion is whether we leave Brandon here alive or dead. It makes little difference to me either way."

"Why on earth would you think that I'd trust your word?" I asked him.

There was a little click as the safety went off. "Perhaps because you understand that it really does not make any difference to me."

"I'll be back in less than fifteen minutes," I said. "I'll call first to be sure that Brandon is all right. Be sure the secretary understands that she's to put my call through."

I felt so wobbly I could barely walk, but I made it down the front hallway and out to the parking lot and got into my car.

When I got back with the burlap-wrapped bundle, I saw Don Marquez's car waiting in front of the school. I knew the man in the driver's seat had to be Sanchez. I sat in the car for a minute in the parking lot, thinking about whether I really wanted to do what I was doing. It still came out the same way, so I went to my office and called on the inside line.

"Let me talk to Brandon," I said when the principal picked up the phone.

"Did you get it?" Brandon asked.

"Are you all right?"

"Sure," he said, "what about you?"

"Of course I got it," I said. "It's just a piece of rather cold rock, after all."

"Right," he said.

When I got to his office, Marquez glanced at the bundle I was carrying and nodded. "My car's here," he said. "Brandon's going to walk right beside me. You go ahead."

I walked out, with the two of them close behind me.

"Carrie and I are going to take Brandon to Oroville,"

Don said to the secretary. "The sheriff is waiting for us. Be sure to remind Hugh about taking detention, will you please? Thank you. See you in the morning, then."

Don's car was a recent model Chrysler with automatic everything. I got into the front beside Sanchez, who didn't look delighted to see me, and Marquez motioned Brandon into the backseat. There was a slight whirring sound as the electric windows slid up, and the electric locks on the doors slid down.

"Did you talk to him?" Don asked Sanchez.

"He'll be there," Sanchez said. "They should have the plane all fueled at the airport, he said. He should get there about the same time we do. The plane won't take five."

"We'll be leaving the boy behind," Marquez said. "The woman will be useful. The United States is so sentimental about its citizens, particularly women."

"I can figure out why you killed Casey," I said, "but why Jensen McGraw? He was your partner, wasn't he?"

"Not at all. McGraw was very helpful, but too short-sighted to look beyond his own interests. When I offered to provide a plane that would bring his little art collection across the border, he never suspected that we had our own purposes. Not until you left that message for him, and then he was full of righteous indignation. We didn't know the Ramos boy had talked to you."

"Queso and Mata are working for you, then?" Brandon asked.

"McGraw's previous driver had an unfortunate accident," Marquez said. "Mata took the position so he could coordinate the art shipments, hold them up until there was currency to bring at the same time."

"So that's what Queso was waiting for at the cove," Brandon said.

"Why did you kill Felipe, if you didn't know he had talked to us?" I asked.

"So he wouldn't have a chance to," Brandon said. "Did you know he'd taken over two thousand dollars?"

"Not until I took the money into San Francisco last night," Marquez said. "The little thief. I told them they couldn't trust him."

We had turned onto the road then into the McGraw Orchards. We rode in silence until we reached the dirt lane leading down toward the shacks and the hay field where the plane would come. Sanchez eased the car expertly over the ruts and rocks. We'd gone perhaps half a mile down the lane when we had to stop because a large branch had blown down and blocked the road.

There was a whirring sound as Sanchez unlocked the door. I noticed that all the door locks had slid up, not just the one on the driver's door. Sanchez got out and began dragging the downed limb out of the way.

"Let me see this treasure that you have," Marquez said to me.

"Ethay oorday isay oay-enpay," I said in a conversational tone as I lifted the burlap bundle to hand to Don across the back of the seat.

"What did you say?" Don asked as he reached forward to take it from me.

Brandon hesitated for maybe two seconds and then he was out of the car. He jumped into the irrigation ditch that ran along the side of the road, and ran crouched over for perhaps twenty-five yards and then cut into the orchard. Don was out the other side and fired two shots after him. Brandon didn't slow down. Both men stood looking after him for a few moments and then got back into the car.

13

I SAT TIED to the one solid chair in the shack and pondered the vagaries of Latin American chauvinism. These two men would roast me alive if the circumstances required, but until that time arrived they would treat me with the solicitous care and automatic deference that they felt was appropriate for my weaker sex and more delicate sensibilities. They had tied me to the chair with great chivalric concern for my comfort, but also with considerable thoroughness.

My wrists were snugly secured to the tubular steel supports of the chair back, at about hip level. My ankles were fastened to the front legs of the chair, snugly, but not so tightly as to cut off the circulation. Don Marquez had consulted me frequently during the process.

"What about that boy?" Sanchez asked. "Where is the plane? It should be here."

"I'm not worried about Brandon Henshaw," Don said. "The boy is well known to be a troublemaker. My reputation in town may decline tomorrow, but as of today any efforts he makes to cry wolf to the authorities will be met with, at best, amusement. And more likely a quick trip back to Juvenile Hall."

Unfortunately, Don was probably right. Brandon would have no trouble convincing the sheriff to pick him up, but anything more than that was doubtful. Still, he was out there somewhere, which seemed our best chance.

"You are staring at me, my dear," Don observed. "Is something the matter?"

"Of course something is the matter," I said. "I am being abducted by someone who has killed three people that I know of personally, and probably many more than that. I was wondering how someone could do that?"

"From your frame of reference," Don said, "it is not possible for you to understand. Your little puppet show of small town morality is what actually makes it all possible, as I said before. If you didn't delude yourselves with certain assumptions, you would have a clearer understanding of the mechanisms through which things occur in the world."

"Assumptions about the value of human life, for instance?"

"At least you understand what I'm talking about," Don said with one of the encouraging smiles he used at faculty meetings when someone had finally proposed the idea that he had wanted to see proposed. "There is no particular value to human life. Only in the quality of life."

"What sort of quality would give it value?" I asked.

"It's something you would have to experience," Don said, and for a moment I felt him as a human being, someone who had some emotional life, some connection with something or someone. "I doubt whether someone of your background would have any way of understanding."

"Try me," I said.

He gave me his sardonic laugh. "You are arrogant," he said. "No matter how limited your actual capacities and experiences, you always think that you can understand. I assure you, from your squalid little life, you cannot. It is unfortunate. You might have been a lady, had you been—"

"To the plantation born?"

"Something like that," he said with a trace of irritation. "It's just a word to you. You really can't understand."

"But it was very beautiful?" I asked.

"Not just that. Cultured. That is what North Americans can never understand because they have no civilization in any genuine sense, so any attempt to describe it they dismiss as pretentious."

"Listen," Sanchez said, "I hear the plane."

We were silent, listening. I heard it, too.

"Get out there," Marquez told him. "Tell him to stay in the plane. We're leaving right away."

"He won't like it," Sanchez said. "You know he says he won't fly out of here until it's nearly dark. Too risky flying for the border in daylight."

"Tell him we don't have any choice this time. Tell him this is the last flight and we have to chance it."

"You know him," Sanchez said. "He's not going to listen to me."

"Tell him I said so. Now get the plane, turn it around for takeoff, and I'll bring her out. Tell him we've got a hostage so they won't try to stop us even if they get suspicious."

Sanchez went out. I could see him through the window. There was a pole, about as tall as a telephone pole, on the edge of the hay field. It had a long strip of white cloth hanging from the top, and I realized it was a makeshift windsock. The plane came over low, and I could see that Sanchez was pointing, with both arms out straight, the direction the wind was coming from. It was blowing toward us from the northeast. Then the plane was out of sight, roaring over the roof, fading off, and then getting louder again. When I saw it, it was coming over so low that I ducked instinctively; the landing wheels seemed to have missed the overhanging eaves by only inches.

The plane touched down about twenty-five yards from the cabins, and taxied to a long low shed at the far end of the field. The plane stopped there. I could see the pilot get out of the plane, could see Sanchez running down the field toward him, waving his arms and shouting something.

They were too far away for me to hear what they were saying, but from the gestures it appeared that they were not in agreement. The pilot seemed to be trying to align the plane with the entrance to the shed, and Sanchez was getting in his way, pointing back toward the shacks. Then both men were coming toward us across the hay field, the pilot ahead, Sanchez following him, still waving his arms.

"The damned fool," Marquez muttered.

The two men burst into the cabin. "I told you I'm not going to fly out of here in daylight," the pilot said.

"I understand your concern," Don said, "and I'm basically in agreement. But this time I'm afraid we have no choice." His voice was as calm as though he were addressing a committee on the prices of school lunches. "You see, there's a chance that we may expect the intervention of the local authorities, and I would like to be gone before that occurs. We have a passenger who will insure our safety. Now, please bring the plane around for takeoff."

I looked out of the window. In the distance, down by the plane and the shed, I saw a figure run across the field from the trees along the river. Whatever was going on out there, it seemed that a diversion might be in order.

"Please leave me here," I burst out. "I won't tell anyone. Please don't hurt me. Don't make me go in the plane."

The men looked at me blankly. I suppose the timing was a bit off, since none of them had been paying any attention to me.

"Don," I said, "please. I'll leave Fair Oaks tonight. I'll never tell anyone. Just don't make me get into the plane. I'm terrified of planes." I kept jabbering, my voice rising hysterically.

"Shut her up," Sanchez said.

"Carrie," Don said, "we are not going to harm you."

"Yes, you are," I wailed. "I know you are. You're going to kill me just like you killed Rick."

"You two get that plane," Marquez said to the others.

"No," I said to Sanchez, "please don't leave me with him. You're a good man, I know you are. Don't leave me with him. He's going to kill me. Please. . . ."

Sanchez started for the door.

"Don't let them hurt me," I begged, turning to the pilot, who was standing there slack-jawed.

I was probably overplaying. At any rate, when Don spoke there was a ring of sudden comprehension in his voice. "Get out to that plane, quick! Here, take this," he said, tossing the gun to Sanchez. "If you see that kid, kill him."

Both of them got to the door simultaneously, jammed up there for a moment, then pushed out. Don walked over to the table where he had left his attaché case and the burlap-wrapped mask. He opened the case, emptied out the papers, and put the mask inside. He took a switchblade from the back compartment, flicked the knife open, and felt the balance of it lying across his palm.

"I'm much more comfortable with this," he said.

The pilot and Sanchez were running across the hay field.

"There's someone out there, isn't there?" Marquez said, moving to the window.

"I hear you're good with that knife," Brandon said from behind us.

Don whirled away from the window. Brandon was

170

standing in the doorway. How could he have gotten down the field so fast?

"Yes," Don said, "but I haven't time for a demonstration." He moved around behind me and put his arm around my neck, pulling my head back. The other hand held the knife against my throat. "Why don't you leave, Brandon? Contrary to some opinions, I do not enjoy killing people if it isn't necessary. There's no reason, outside of the fact that you have been very irritating this afternoon, why I should kill you. There's no need for it."

"He's right, Brandon," I said. "Go on. They won't hurt me. They need me alive to be sure they won't be stopped."

"You remember what we said we wanted?" Brandon said. "Do you still want it?"

"I want you alive," I said.

"Do you still want it?"

"Brandon, he'll kill you. You said you're not that good. You told me that."

"You'll give him a psychological advantage saying that," Brandon said. "Do you still want it?"

He was looking at me and I was looking at him. Did I want it that much? To have him make an effort that didn't stand a chance?

"Yes," I said, bracing my feet as solidly as I could on the floor, and then pushing back with all the strength and leverage I could manage.

For a moment Marquez was off balance, holding the entire weight of me and the tipped chair with his left elbow. Then with a sudden backward step he half dropped and half shoved me so that I sprawled to the floor, the chair on top of me, my arms wrenched up painfully behind. I managed to wedge the chair against the iron bedstead and get into a kneeling position, and then back to being on the chair instead of under it. But I couldn't get free from it. They had tied me too securely for that. I heard the roar of the plane engine.

Brandon had moved into the room. Marquez was moving toward him, slowly, crouched slightly, moving the knife easily from one hand to the other. He didn't toss the knife from one hand to another but brought his hands together. Less flash but more control.

The only advantage that Brandon had was that he was younger, lighter, faster on his feet. He made a couple of feints as though to grab for the knife, and Marquez stopped moving forward. Suddenly Brandon stepped backward and to the side, grabbing one of the old blankets down from the rafters. He held it doubled, both ends in one hand, so it formed a thick, heavy fabric loop, which he swung through the air in an arc. Marquez, surprised, spread his arms to avoid tangling them in the blanket, and as he did, Brandon lunged at him, dropping the blanket and grabbing the arm that held the knife.

They both went down, grappling on the floor, Brandon holding onto Don's right wrist with both hands, pounding it against the table leg to loosen his grip on the knife. Marquez had Brandon around the neck with his other arm and was yanking his head back. And then suddenly with a twisting motion Brandon had the knife and broke free and they both scrambled to their feet.

"That's good," Don said, "very good. But you really don't know how to kill with it, do you? You're not really sure, are you?"

"Don't worry," Brandon said, "I know." He held the knife low, hardly a foot above the floor, taking every advantage he could of being more agile than the older man.

Suddenly Marquez moved, faster than I would have thought he could, to Brandon's left, away from the knife. Instead of turning toward him, Brandon whirled backward, pivoting and bringing the knife up and out. It slashed across the calf of Don's leg, drawing blood that stained the cut pants leg slowly. It wasn't a deep cut.

Don jumped back. "Good," he said. "You really have wasted your talents. But you can't kill, can you?"

I could tell that he was right, and that Brandon knew it. "Maybe not," Brandon said, "but the next cut will put you down."

He moved in again, low again, and this time Marquez only feinted to the left and then lunged for Brandon, throwing his right shoulder into Brandon's chest and grabbing for the hand that held the knife.

Then Sanchez came in behind them with the gun, the pilot behind him. As Sanchez hit Brandon from behind with the butt of the gun, Marquez twisted the knife away from him. I saw the knife come up, the blood come red through Brandon's shirt and the half-open jacket as he slumped forward to the floor.

"Brandon," I cried, "Brandon, no. No!"

And then the explosion came, sounding like a cannon in that small space. Sanchez and the pilot froze. The only one who moved was Marquez, who had had the left side of his face half blown away by both barrels of Tim Jordan's twelve-gauge fired at very close range through the window.

"Bring the woman," Sanchez said to the pilot. "Get to the plane."

They cut me loose and dragged me out and around the corner of the cabin. Tim Jordan was still by the window, bent over the shotgun, trying to reload. I was between the two men, half running, half being dragged over the muddy uneven ground. I could hear sirens. I thought that I would not get into the plane, but Sanchez twisted my arm and jerked it up behind my back so that the pain was stronger than the thought had been. Also, I had the feeling that nothing mattered very much.

The plane was a four-seater. Sanchez boosted me up

and shoved me in beside the pilot and climbed over into the back. Then we were jolting and bouncing down the hay field, the engine roaring, the plane accelerating until it suddenly broke free from the ground and into its element, the bright April air.

I heard a distant report, and turned a little in the seat to see that Tim had fired after the plane in frustration. Past the receding shacks I could see the sheriff's car bouncing down the lane. It looked like a toy car.

"There's a first-aid kit with some ether back there," the pilot said. "If she causes any trouble, put her out."

"Don't bother," I said. "I like flying, actually."

I did. I liked the sight of the earth moving away, the odd perspective of being above it rather than on it. I had never been plagued by imagining that airplanes might not stay up in the air. Their function was to go up in the air and stay there until someone decided it was time for them to go down again, and in my experience they had always done that.

Therefore, when the engine suddenly stopped and the plane lurched and shuddered in the air, I assumed it was only a small aberration of some sort. The engine coughed and started again, and then stopped again. Even as the plane nosed over and I was looking directly at the mass of trees along the river bank, I still expected that the plane would right itself in a moment.

"No es posible," I heard the pilot say. "There's no fuel."

The trees were very close, and were beginning to wheel, or seemed to, because the plane was turning as it descended. I could see the young green leaves very clearly. They were right by the window. And then we were into them and I heard the crunching before I felt it. When I felt it, it came hard and fast and I didn't see or feel anything else.

14

WHEN I WOKE up, it was slowly, from a dream that someone was stabbing me over and over and over again. I knew I was waking up, because sometimes I knew it was a dream, since I'd be dead from that much stabbing if it weren't.

When I opened my eyes, I closed them again. I was in a white room, and bright sunlight was coming in a window. I opened them a little. Enough to see that someone was standing by the window looking out. When I breathed in, I understood why I had been having that dream. Breathing hurt. I had made a sound when it hurt, because the person at the window turned around and came toward the bed.

"Awake, are you?" the sheriff asked. "I just stopped in to see if you might be coming around."

I tried to ask him something, but the amount of breath that it took to prepare to say something was more than I really wanted to take, so I didn't. It didn't seem important, anyway.

"The doctor said you shouldn't try to talk," the sheriff said. I had figured that out on my own. "He says you've got a couple of cracked ribs there. Beside the leg."

When he said that I was aware of a dull ache in my right leg. I tried to move my legs. One of them moved and one of them didn't. I looked down, without moving anything except my eyes, and saw a white bulge about where I would have expected my right leg to be.

"Where?" I asked, proving that I could say one syllable words with the amount of breath I had to breathe out anyway.

"Don't talk," he said. "You're in the hospital in Oroville. Broken leg, cracked ribs, dislocated collarbone, black eye, lots of bruises, but Dr. Lampson seems to think a little mending will put you back about in the same condition you were in before the crash."

I remembered the leaves then, coming up toward the plane. "When?"

"It's Thursday morning now. They said you'd be coming out of the sedation. Don't talk. You are not a patient woman, Miz Pritchard," he said, intercepting the question I had for the next breath. "If you'll be still, I'll tell you."

I turned my head toward the window, which gave me a verification of his information about the collarbone. My eyes were adjusting to the brightness of the room. The window was open and the white curtains moved gently. I could feel the freshness of the air. Dear God, it was all going to keep going on, whether I wanted it to or not. It seemed more horrible that this was so than anything that had gone before.

"Sanchez and the Mexican who was flying the plane are both beat up pretty bad like you are," the sheriff said, "but they're alive. Sanchez has been talking, as a matter of fact. Seems Marquez was one of Somoza's right-hand men before the revolution in Nicaragua. Afterwards, everyone thought he was dead. Well, he is now. That X ray matches up with what was left of his face, by the way.

"For a while he was with the contras in Honduras, hoping to get back in power. It was slow dirty work, though. Not his style. I guess he figured there must be an easier way, and then he figured what it was. A few of them started siphoning off the money that was coming into Honduras for military support. They set up an

176

operation to get the currency to Mexico by boat, and then into the US by plane. Once they had it set up, they found a lot of interested clients who wanted to have their assets invested in this country.

"Marquez had a partner in San Francisco who handled the investments. He got out on a commercial flight before we could get to him. The Mexican police got Queso and Mata, though. They don't give a damn one way or another about the funds for the contras, but they get real efficient when their national treasures are involved."

It didn't seem to matter one way or another. Odd, I thought, when you want something, and you get it . . . it's just an ending. I closed my eyes.

"I'll get the doctor," Pratcher said. "He's just down the hall. If there's anything else, I'll tell you later."

In a moment I heard steps coming in. "I was afraid you were dead," he said. I turned my head quickly. It hurt a lot but I didn't mind.

"I was sure you were," I said, and I didn't mind the breath it took, either, "—until right now."

Brandon hopped up on the end of the bed, which made it shake, which hurt some more.

"Oops," he said. "Sorry."

I found I could move my hand a bit, and he reached for it and held it. I could cry without moving anything, and I did.

"Does it hurt that much?" he asked.

"No," I said. "No."

"I was just knocked out for a couple of minutes," Brandon said. "I didn't know you thought I was dead. I saw the plane crash. Tim got most of the gasoline out, but he couldn't get it all. They had enough to take off."

So it had been Tim down by the plane, not Brandon. "Blood," I said.

"On me? Just a little. I got a couple of Sam Jordan's wide leather belts when I was up at their house. I went there as soon as I got out of the car. Tim called the sheriff and got his dad's shotgun and we went down to the shacks. Anyway, I put a couple of those leather belts around my ribs under the jacket, just in case. The knife slid off one of them and made a little cut. Nothing serious. Four or five stitches."

I squeezed his hand and just held it.

"Orange juice seems to work OK," he said.

Then the room was full of people. A nurse who shooed Brandon off the end of the bed in a flurry of righteous indignation. Dr. Lampson, who was checking my pulse. The sherifff again. Virgil Henshaw, who took the occasion to deliver a little speech.

"I'm a drunk," he said earnestly. "I nearly lost my boy, and it brought me to my knees to ask the Lord for help. I'm going to make it up to him. We're going to go fishing, do things together."

Virgil looked better than I'd ever seen him, the color in his face natural, his hair cut neatly, his eyes a little watery, but clear.

"I'll wait in the truck for you, boy," he said, and went out.

"The house is clean," Brandon said.

"Sometimes they make it," the sheriff said. "He's been going to the A.A. meetings here in town."

"I'm not sure I can handle this," Brandon said, looking a little desperate.

"You'll do OK," the sheriff said.

"I just hope I can catch a fish," Brandon said.

If you have enjoyed this book and would like to receive
details of other Walker mystery titles, please write to:

Mystery Editor
Walker and Company
720 Fifth Avenue
New York, NY 10019